Resurgence 2030

A POST-APOCALYPTIC FICTION

A Novel By

NASH NIAZ
Award-Winning Screenwriter

ISBN: 979-8-218-53839-2
Virtualwords Publishing

This novel is entirely a work of fiction.
The names, characters, and incidents portrayed
in the book are the work of the author's imagination.
Any resemblance to actual persons, living or dead,
events or localities, is purely coincidental.

WGAW Registration: 2266483
Printed in the United States of America

ABOUT THE AUTHOR

From the visionary mind of screenwriter Nash Niaz comes Resurgence 2030, a genre-bending masterpiece of post-apocalyptic fiction. Based on his critically acclaimed screenplay, this gripping novel takes readers on an unforgettable journey through action, faith, and the unyielding human spirit. Are you ready to embark on your resurgence?

Nash Niaz is an award-winning screenwriter whose storytelling brilliance transcends mediums. His critically acclaimed screenplay, Resurgence 2030, has garnered international recognition, winning awards and nominations at prestigious film festivals such as the Nice International Film Festival (France), Los Angeles Stars Film Festival, Swedish International Film Festival, Switzerland International Film Festival, Screenwriters Network's Screenplay Awards (UK), New York City International Screenplay Awards, San Francisco International Screenwriting Awards, Sacramento International Film Festival, Austin Action Film Festival, Hollywood International Diversity Film Festival, Miami Screenplay Awards, Scriptmatix Screenplay Awards, Santa Barbara International Screenplay Awards, and many more.

DEDICATION

To all those who endure in a world scarred by wars,
genocides, terrorism, hunger, and homelessness. May these
pages honor your resilience and remind the world of the
immutable light within each of you.

ACKNOWLEDGMENTS

Writing this novel has been a profound journey. I am deeply thankful to everyone who supported me along the way. My heartfelt gratitude goes to my family and friends for their unwavering love, encouragement, and patience throughout this process. Finally, I extend my deepest gratitude to the readers who have joined me on this journey. Your support means more than words can convey.

1 WAR-TORN SANCTUARY

California, 2030. An old, weathered farmhouse stood deep in the woods, hidden from the outside world. A twisting coastline and layered mountains surrounded the little valley. Near the shore, swarms of seagulls rested on a shell-damaged abandoned ship.

In the distance, the faint rumblings of gunfire and throbbing explosions echo from the cities. The courtyard and barn bear the scars of stray shells. Behind the farmhouse, a private cemetery lay nestled in the quiet refuge of the landscape.

Davina, a grief-stricken woman in her late 20s, knelt beside a headstone that read, "Your memory lives on, our dearest daughter Emma."

Sebastian, her husband, a rugged farmer in his early 30s, walked up and sat beside her. He sighed deeply and wrapped his arm gently around Davina. Her body trembled with silent sobs. They sat in silence for a long while, lost in their grief.

As the morning sun rose on the horizon, Davina stepped out of the front porch and headed toward an old stable standing at the edge of the property. She diligently cleaned the stable. A malnourished horse named Astro stood in one corner of the stable, the ribs visible beneath its coat. Davina filled a small bucket with a meager amount of horse feed.

"Sorry, that's all I have for now," said Davina.

She watched the horse with affectionate eyes. Astro looked up at her with pleading eyes. She leaned in, wrapping her arms around his neck.

"I know it's been tough, but we'll find a way to make things better," Davina said.

With a heavy sigh, she closed the stable gate and walked toward the courtyard.

2 A BEACON OF HOPE EMERGES

The serene sound of birds chirping was disrupted by the distant echoes of gunfire, tearing through the tranquility. Sebastian and Davina loaded bushels of corn and ripe tomatoes onto a pickup truck with faded paint.

"Most folks are leaving," said Davina.

"We can't abandon this farm now," Sebastian replied.

Davina secured the bushels with a tattered truck cover and walked over to Sebastian.

"I know how much this farm means to you, but the city is crumbling around us," Davina said.

Sebastian replied, "Where the hell can we go? Besides, there's still a demand for our crops in the market. Let's head out first thing in the morning."

"We should get back before sundown. It's not safe to be out there after dark," Davina said.

Sebastian replied, "We'll make it back before nightfall."

Sebastian closed the truck's tailgate.

They hopped into the truck. Sebastian drove along the perimeter of their farmhouse toward the dirt road blocked by a tangle of tree branches and scattered rocks. They cleared the path and drove across to the other side, then put the tree branches and rocks back. Sebastian sped out onto the highway. He cautiously approached the outskirts of the city as Davina sat in tense silence.

"It's getting worse every day," said Sebastian.

Davina looked around at the grim surroundings in disbelief. A war-torn city lay in ruins as artillery explosions reverberated through the air. She clutched Sebastian's arm tightly, her eyes filled with fear and despair. Dreadful flames and plumes of smoke rose from ragged piles of rubble and smoldering vehicles. A swarm of cars, SUVs, and pickup trucks swerved through the debris-littered roads.

Sebastian spotted three military vehicles with dark-clad separatist rebels, emerging ominously from a back road onto the highway. Uniformed government forces in combat vehicles with fluttering US flags chased the rebels, firing their machine guns.

Shouting and indistinct instructions can be heard amid explosions. The rebels fired back with RPGs, blowing up one of the government vehicles. The remaining government forces retaliated, firing rockets at the rebels, leaving trails of smoke in their wake. Two of the rebel vehicles were struck, exploding in the middle of the highway, and erupting into a ball of flames. A series of crashes ensue, fire and ash everywhere.

A sedan in front of Sebastian's truck spun out of control. Its tires screeched against the asphalt. The sedan lurched off course and collided violently with a van. The sedan's driver, a nineteen-year-old woman, stunned and disoriented, screamed as her car flipped over, skidding into the roadside ditch.

Sebastian instinctively slammed on the brakes, trying desperately to regain control of his vehicle. Davina's eyes widened in horror as she gazed at the sedan trapped in the ditch.

The young woman slowly crawled halfway out of the vehicle. Her face was bloody and bruised. Her left leg remained trapped inside the crushed car, a stream of blood gushing out of her abdomen. She pulled her injured two-year-old boy out of the vehicle. The toddler wept as the blood from her abdomen soaked his clothes.

"Hold on, sweetie, we'll get out of here," the young mother said. She tried to free her trapped leg, groaning in pain. The toddler cried, his hands gripping onto his mother's clothes, tears and blood on his face. The mother collapsed onto the ground, her vision fading. She tried to whisper some words as she took her last breath, still clutching the toddler.

"Mommy, mommy," the toddler cried out.

Suddenly, a blinding divine light glowed around the toddler, casting a warm glow across the desolate scene. He stumbled to his feet, taking unsteady steps, as broken glass cut into his feet. He fell onto the ground, his body quivering with pain. Slowly, he rose and walked back to his mother's side. He picked up his tattered teddy bear from the ground. Clutching it tightly, he wrapped his arms around his mother's lifeless body.

Davina and Sebastian stared at the glowing toddler. Sebastian pulled the truck over to the side of the road. Davina jumped out of the truck and rushed toward the ditch, Sebastian following closely behind. As they approached the toddler, Davina and Sebastian were engulfed in the bright light. They were awestruck in stunned disbelief as the aura grew brighter. Davina gazed at the little boy with wonder in her eyes, still in a state of shock.

"My God, my God," Davina exclaimed.

She crouched down and picked up the sobbing boy. The toddler screamed. Sebastian bent over beside the mother's lifeless body, checking for a pulse. He spotted a small bag lying next to the mother's corpse. He picked it up and discovered a smartphone amidst baby accessories.

"What're we gonna do with him?" asked Sebastian, his gaze lingering on the smartphone.

Davina walked toward their truck holding the toddler against her chest as he screamed.

"We can't leave him here. We can keep him," replied Davina.

Sebastian stared at Davina, her face emanating warmth as she soothed the sobbing toddler. Davina got into the back seat holding the toddler in her arms. Sebastian turned the truck around and drove forward hastily.

3 A SHELTER OF LOVE
IN A WORLD OF CHAOS

As they arrived at their farmhouse, Davina gently removed the toddler's blood-soaked clothes, revealing minor bruises and scratches. She reached for a first-aid kit and began applying bandages as he winced and sobbed.

Davina whispered, "You're safe now, sweetie, we're here to protect you."

On the TV screen, a journalist in her 30s reported the news updates, her voice carrying a sense of despair.

"The civil war continues to escalate, with Southern and Northern separatists, Neo-Nazi extremists, and anti-government militias seizing control of several towns in Texas."

Sebastian's face turned grim, his brows furrowing with worry, as he listened to the distressing news.

The reporter continued, "The persistent ethnic tensions, territorial disputes, and resource conflicts in Asia and the Middle East remain a source of immense human suffering, resulting in devastating casualties."

The toddler gradually calmed down as Davina cradled him in her arms. Sebastian unzipped the small bag and picked up the smartphone. He pressed the phone's power button, revealing the cover image of the toddler in his mother's arms.

Sebastian scrolled through a series of pictures. Davina leaned in and glanced at the photos. The caption read,

"Matthew's First Birthday."

Davina held the toddler even tighter. "In all this darkness, he's a little miracle," said Davina.

Sebastian leaned closer to Davina, wrapping his arm around her. They gazed at the toddler's innocent face as their eyes sparkled with love and wonder.

4 LOVE & FRIENDSHIP
IN THE FACE OF ADVERSITY

Thirteen years later…

A small cottage stood behind the farmhouse of Davina and Sebastian. Analia Garcia, a thirteen-year-old girl with long, flowing hair, entered the kitchen.

Her aunt Sophia, a woman in her late 40s with a kind face marked by years of struggles, stirred a pot of simmering soup.

Analia asked, "Aunt Sophia, I was wondering…can Matthew have dinner with us tonight?"

Sophia replied, "Sure, honey." Analia nodded, momentarily embracing her aunt, then turned toward the door. Sophia smiled, staring at her, her eyes brimming with affection.

Matthew, now 15, had grown up to be a slender young man, taller for his age, with light brown shoulder-length wavy hair. He worked on a raft with pieces of logs and wood. The distant sound of sirens and gunfire reverberated through the air, creating an unsettling contrast with the peaceful symphony of crickets. Analia walked over to Matthew and held his arm. She looked at the raft. Excitement sparkled in her eyes.

"I can't wait to try it," Analia said.

Matthew paused momentarily, assessing his progress, then looked at Analia.

"I think it will be ready by sundown tomorrow," replied Matthew.

Analia smiled warmly and leaned closer to Matthew.

She said, "You can have dinner with us, I'll help Auntie prepare."

Matthew nodded with a smile. Analia turned and headed back toward her house. Matthew returned his attention to work, and his focus renewed.

5 FOR MATTHEW'S FUTURE:
A PROMISE AMIDST RUINS

Inside the farmhouse, a collage of Matthew's baby pictures showcased the passage of time. Davina and Sebastian gracefully embraced middle age, their hair greyed to salt and pepper. Sitting on a worn-out couch, they watched the news updates on television, interrupted by intermittent power outages.

A reporter in her 40s stood amid the chaos of dreadful gunfire and billowing smoke. The footage showed unsettling scenes of mass graves and morgues. The screen transitioned to images of ruined wildlife, shattered by devastating quakes and raging volcanoes. Davina and Sebastian watched the news with stunned silence, their faces filled with sadness and disbelief.

"How did the world let it go on for so long?" Davina whispered.

"It feels like we've been sinking deeper into this hole with no end in sight," Sebastian replied. Davina sighed deeply.

"We have to survive. We must find a way... for Matthew... for his future," said Davina.

6 NATURE'S PLAYMATES

Matthew led a Kentucky Mountain Saddle horse toward the shoreline. The sun glared over the soft sand as waves crashed against the shore. Analia ran up to Matthew and rested her head on his shoulder. He helped her onto the back of the horse.

"I'll race you to the water's edge," Matthew said.

Analia giggled as the horse ran against the crashing tides. Matthew ran alongside. The vast expanse of the ocean stretched out behind them. After a while, Matthew slowed down and stopped near the shore. He walked into the water and dove down, disappearing momentarily. He resurfaced, holding a few small fish in his hands. Intrigued, Analia got off the horse and joined Matthew in the water.

"How did you catch them with your bare hands?" Analia asked.

Matthew grinned and tugged Analia deeper into the water. He pointed to a small hole in the shallow sea floor camouflaged by a layer of weeds. His hand reached into the concealed hole and skillfully retrieved a tiny fish. Analia eagerly reached out to another hole nearby, mimicking the technique she had just witnessed. With a swift motion, she captured a small fish in her grasp. Emerging triumphantly from the water, Analia proudly tossed her catch onto the shore. A beaming smile adorned her face.

A flock of ducks spotted the flipping fish on the beach and moved toward it. Matthew and Analia waded out of the water and walked onto the shore, leaving wet footprints behind.

Analia's aunt's voice carried from the distance.

"Anna, I need you here."

Analia's face fell with disappointment.

"I have to go now," Analia said.

She quickly kissed Matthew on the cheek, then ran toward the cottage, her hair flowing behind. Matthew turned to the horse and mounted it, urging it to gallop toward a small hill.

7 DREAMS OF CRUCIFIXION

Matthew slept on the bed, tossing and turning. He slipped into a deep dream. He found himself in a desolate landscape, gradually transforming into a tall man with long hair and an untrimmed beard. He wore a torn robe, barely covering his blood-soaked skin. A massive wooden cross rested heavily on his shoulders as he stumbled and fell to the ground.

He saw a divine hand reaching out, gently wiping away the blood and sweat. He saw himself nailed on a two-beamed cross, his arms stretched, fingernails streaming in blood. A wrinkled, hairy hand put a crown of thorns on his tortured head while others pierced him with thorny spears, tearing off his flesh at every blow.

Matthew screamed out.

"My God, my God!"

His body shivered and flinched. He woke up, sweating and shaking with heavy, desperate breathing.

Davina and Sebastian rushed into his room, seeing him curled up on the bed. Davina sat down and comforted him, wrapping her arms around him.

"It's just a bad dream, sweetie," Davina said.

Matthew's voice quivered, his breaths still heavy with fear.

"They put me on the cross," said Matthew.

Davina's eyes met Sebastian's. She leaned in and kissed

Matthew's forehead. Sitting on the other side of Matthew, Sebastian extended his hand and gently ran his fingers through his hair, offering a comforting touch.

8 A SUPERPOWER REVEALED

Matthew walked aimlessly on the desolate beach, his face clouded with melancholy and distress. Analia walked up to him and stared at his face.

"What's wrong?" asked Analia.

Matthew replied, "Nothing….!"

They hauled the raft into the water and swiftly embarked, rowing toward the partially sunken ship looming in the distance. They arrived at the decaying ship and cautiously stepped onto the creaking deck, exploring its eerie interior that evoked a sense of mystery and danger.

After a while, they returned on the raft and rowed toward a low hill near the shore. They arrived at the base of the mountain, where Matthew ascended with Analia closely trailing behind him. They strolled together, exploring their surroundings before settling down at the entrance of a cave. Matthew leaned in, gently kissing her as she embraced him tightly. After a brief pause, Matthew's gaze became fixated on the source of gunfire, resonating in the distance.

"It's hard to believe from here that the world is falling apart," Matthew said.

"I'm so glad we stayed here," said Analia.

"This is the only place where I truly feel at peace," Matthew said. They sat there in silence as the sun set over the horizon.

After a long while, Analia said, "We should go…"

They began their descent down the hill. Analia followed Matthew but slipped and tumbled. As she hit the ground, she instinctively grasped her left ankle, which was now seeping blood.

Matthew rushed to her side, and with gentle care, he used his hand to clean the sand from her injured ankle. Analia stared at her ankle, and to her astonishment, the wounds began to heal. As Matthew continued, the wounds were healed completely. Analia burst out in awe, captivated.

"How did you do that?" asked Analia.

Matthew laid her ankle down as he stared at the healed wounds in disbelief.

"My God! It seems like a real superpower," exclaimed Analia. Matthew was visibly dizzy, shaking his head.

Analia asked, "Are you ok?"

Matthew, regaining his composure, helped Analia stand. They walked toward the farmhouse.

9 A RUTHLESS LEADER RISES

The US President, Harrison Williams, a man in his 60s with a temperamental and ruthless demeanor, met with several leaders. The wall screens displayed chaotic footage of the civil war and foreign wars. NSA Director Hudson Collin, a self-controlled, sixty-four-year-old bald man with intense eyes, addressed the President.

"Mr. President, our foreign wars are causing rifts in NATO. Our allies are questioning our actions, and it's affecting our global standing," said Collin.

President Williams' face turned red with anger as he interrupted.

"NATO can go to hell! I don't need those cowards telling me how to run our country," said President Williams.

Vice President Clara Madison, a woman in her late 50s, appeared distraught.

"Mr. President, the civil war is tearing the nation apart, and people are blaming you for instigating this chaos," Madison said. President Williams rose from his seat.

"They don't understand what it takes to maintain power and control," said President Williams. Vice President Madison's voice quivered.

"Sir, we need to find a way to end the conflicts," Madison said.

She locked eyes with NSA Director Collin, silently pleading for support.

"Mr. President, I think we should prioritize stability now," said Collin.

President Williams paced, his expression unyielding.

"We can't let sentimentality cloud our vision," President Williams said.

10 RESTLESS NIGHT IN NATURE

Matthew lay restless on his bed, tossing and turning, glancing at the clock on the side table. It read 1:00 AM. He rose from his bed and gazed out the window, then stepped out. He strolled along the beach and reached the foot of a nearby hill, lush with foliage. He settled beneath a massive tree, finding solace and a sense of calmness.

After a few peaceful moments, several wild foxes emerged from the forest, their eyes gleaming with curiosity. Drawn to Matthew's divine aura, they cautiously approached him. They gathered around him, lying near his feet. Matthew's face lit up with a gentle smile. He leaned his head against the trunk of the tree. His breath became steady and calm as he entered a peaceful slumber.

As the morning sun rose over the tranquil landscape, Sebastian set the table while Davina cooked breakfast, their faces marked with deep concern.

"Is Matthew's insomnia getting better?" asked Sebastian.

Davina looked worried, sighing deeply.

"No, if anything, it's getting worse. It's triggering his anxiety," replied Davina.

Sebastian took a deep breath and poured coffee into three cups. He then headed for Matthew's bedroom. He stood outside Matthew's bedroom door, knocking gently. There was no response. He opened the door slowly and peered inside, then looked out the window. There was no sign of Matthew. Sebastian stepped out. He walked toward the nearby mountains, his eyes scanning the surroundings.

He called out, "Matthew."

He arrived at the base of a hill. His gaze fell on a breathtaking sight. Bathed in a divine radiance, Matthew slept peacefully underneath the tree. Sebastian moved closer, his eyes widened in astonishment. He spotted two wild bears lying next to Matthew, their presence both intimidating and awe-inspiring.

"My God!" Sebastian exclaimed.

He reached behind his back and pulled out a handgun. The bears lifted their heads briefly before resting them next to Matthew's shoulders. Sebastian's hand trembled. Slowly, he put the gun behind his back, realizing the peaceful intent of the bears. He sat across from Matthew, his eyes fixed on the dazzling light emanating from his son's body.

11 WHISPERS OF PROPHECY

Davina and Sebastian sat together, their eyes fixed on the television screen. A news anchor in her 30s addressed the studio camera.

"As years of turmoil and unrest bring the world to ruin, religious leaders point to the signs of the End Times," read the news anchor.

Sebastian's eyes narrowed with concern, his voice heavy with worry. He reached for the remote control, switching off the TV.

"I wonder about Matthew, we witnessed his powers," Sebastian said.

Davina's gaze shifted from the television to Sebastian, her face etched with worry lines.

"It scares me to think about it, but it's always been on my mind," Davina said.

"If he's the one, we have to nurture him until he's ready. We must guide him toward his purpose," Sebastian said.

"But what if he's just a boy with special abilities?" asked Davina. Sebastian's gaze met Davina's, his voice steady and resolute.

"Even if he's not the Second Coming, we must help him understand his divine powers," said Sebastian. Davina nodded, her worry slowly transforming into conviction.

12 THE CALL OF DESTINY

Matthew, now in his early 20s, with a bearded face and long hair, tossed and turned in bed. His body flinched in his sleep. He suddenly awoke. He got up and rushed out of his room, slamming the door behind him. He ran along the beach, panic evident on his face. A distant siren blared, piercing the night.

Sebastian awoke from the sound. He got up quietly and headed toward Matthew's room. He entered the room. His gaze shifted to the window, witnessing Matthew's frantic run on the water.

Sebastian rushed out the door. As he leaped toward the beach, he spotted Matthew moving further into the sea. Sebastian screamed, his voice filled with desperation.

"Matthew!" Sebastian called.

In her room, Analia awoke. She looked out the window, her eyes widening in disbelief. She saw Matthew running frantically on the water's surface.

"Dear Lord," exclaimed Analia.

Sebastian dove into the water. Matthew swiftly pivoted, his eyes brimming with confusion. Sebastian reached Matthew, catching him as his energy waned. Matthew collapsed, splashing into the water, and began to sink. Sebastian fought against the water, pulling Matthew to the shore.

Matthew's eyes fluttered open, weakened and disoriented. Sebastian helped him sit up.

"What's happening to me, Dad?" Matthew whispered.

Sebastian wrapped his arm around Matthew, comforting him.

"I think you were sent here to heal the world, son. Maybe you're the one the world's been waiting for," said Sebastian.

"I just want to lead a simple life," Matthew said.

"I believe your path is chosen for you. If you are the one, God will guide you," said Sebastian.

"Why would the world believe in me?" asked Matthew.

Sebastian gazed at his son, his eyes etched with conviction.

"I think when the world is ready, it will believe," replied Sebastian.

"What if you are wrong and I'm not the one?" Matthew asked.

"I believe everything will be revealed to you in due time," Sebastian replied.

He placed a hand on Matthew's shoulder with a reassuring smile.

13 REVEALING THE PAST: MATTHEW'S ROOTS

Matthew sat on the floor, his back leaning against the couch. Sitting on the sofa, Davina stroked his hair tenderly. Sebastian came out from the bedroom, holding a small cell phone. Taking a deep breath he sat down beside Matthew.

"Matthew, there's something we should have shown you," said Sebastian.

The cell phone screen showed a baby picture of Matthew with his birth mother. Shocked and confused, Matthew scrolled through the phone, finding a video of his mother singing "Happy Birthday" to him. Matthew stared at his parents, his voice trembling.

"Why have you waited until now?" asked Matthew.

Davina and Sebastian remained quiet for a moment, gathering their thoughts. Davina leaned closer to Matthew, her voice breaking slightly.

"We were waiting… for the right time," replied Davina. Matthew's eyes welled up with tears.

"Why… why did she leave me?" Matthew asked.

"Your mother saved your life. She passed away in an accident, and we brought you home," Sebastian replied.

"And… my father?" Matthew asked.

Sebastian's gaze dropped, a sadness washed over him.

"We couldn't trace your father or any other relatives,

Matthew," said Sebastian.

Davina wrapped her arm around Matthew, tears glistening in her eyes.

"You're our son, Matthew. We've always loved you as our own," said Davina.

14 UNVEILING DIVINE POWERS

Analia, now 21, virtuously elegant, soft-spoken, and affectionate, sat with Matthew on the soft silver sand. After a moment, Matthew broke the silence.

"Did you get to know your parents?" asked Matthew.

"I barely remember their faces. They died in the war," replied Analia. Matthew sighed deeply.

"I never got to know mine," said Matthew.

"What do you mean?" Analia asked.

"My birth parents..." Matthew replied.

Matthew retrieved the worn cell phone from his pocket and showed her his birthday pictures. Analia looked at the pictures, holding his arm affectionately.

"They've always loved you as their son," said Analia.

Matthew nodded and paused, taking a deep breath.

"Lately, I've been haunted by strange dreams, where I find myself crucified, just like Jesus..." said Matthew.

Analia's eyes widened in surprise.

"My God! That's terrifying..." said Analia.

Matthew remained silent as they strolled along the beach. Analia turned to Matthew, a blend of curiosity and amusement playing across her face.

"Can you show me how you walk on the water?" asked Analia.

Matthew smiled warmly and took a moment, considering

her request. As they reached the water's edge, Matthew paused. Holding Analia in his arms, he stepped forward, his foot hovering just above the water's surface. With serene focus, he set his foot on the water. He continued walking, effortlessly gliding across the water's surface. Analia's eyes widened in astonishment and sheer joy.

"Matthew, this is incredible! Maybe the world's ready for a divine superhero," she said.

"But I'm not ready," said Matthew.

"I know divine power is a heavy burden. It's beyond our understanding," said Analia.

"I have doubts, but I want to have faith," Matthew said.

"I don't know if I'm ready to let you go on your path," Analia said.

Analia tightened her arms around Matthew, kissing him passionately.

15 MATTHEW'S INNER TURMOIL: CONFRONTING DOUBTS

Matthew sat on the porch, absorbed in a book. Davina took a seat beside him, her expression heavy with anguish.

"We know you have a divine calling, Matthew. But the weight of it all, the uncertainty and risks involved, it worries me to death," said Davina.

Matthew closed the book, a calm and compassionate look in his eyes.

"I keep wondering, mother, one part of me wants to believe this is my purpose. Then again, the doubts and the fears are always hanging over me," said Matthew.

Davina leaned her head against his shoulder, her voice trembling.

"If you are the Second Coming, what will stop them from crucifying you again?" asked Davina.

Sebastian emerged from the storage, holding a drill in his hand.

"If Revelation 16:14 is right, the kings and the rulers of the world will be dealt with by God," said Sebastian.

"I want him to have a peaceful life, he doesn't have to be the world's savior," said Davina.

"It's not his choice... the signs of the apocalypse are all around us. With time, God will prepare him for his journey," said Sebastian.

"I don't know, Dad, I'm torn between the paths…" said Matthew.

"All prophecies point to this century when the Second Coming is to occur. If I'm wrong about your path, no harm is done. But, if I'm right, you must be ready to receive divine guidance. Let's pray…" Sebastian led a silent prayer.

Suddenly, Analia rushed in, her face filled with tension and distress. Matthew and his parents instinctively rose to their feet, gripped by a collective gasp.

"What's wrong, Ana?" asked Matthew. Analia's voice trembled with emotion.

"Aunt Sophie got shot by stray bullets," said Analia.

"Oh God…no…no…" screamed Davina.

16 MATTHEW THE HEALER

As they arrived at the hospital, land and air ambulances dropped off dozens of injured men and women. With sadness etched on his face, Matthew stared at them for a moment, some of them screaming in pain.

They strode into the emergency room where Sophia lay unconscious, with bandages around her head and arm. A female doctor and a male nurse administered oxygen while trying to stop the bleeding. Analia sat by Sophia's bedside, weeping and holding her hand. Matthew put his arm around Analia, trying to comfort her.

"Can you… can you try healing her?" asked Analia.

Matthew hesitated for a moment, then nodded with determination. He placed his right hand on Sophia's wound. The wound healed as Sophia stirred, her eyes fluttered open. Analia pulled Sophia into a warm embrace, tenderly wiping away her tears.

The doctor and the nurse gazed at the miraculously healed wound with utter astonishment. The doctor turned to Matthew, her voice filled with awe and hope.

"Can you help us? Can you heal others?" asked the doctor.

Matthew's gaze shifted from the doctor to Analia and Sophia.

"We'll be ok," said Analia.

The doctor led Matthew to a bed where a young man in his 20s lay in pain. His mother tightly clutched his hand. Matthew laid his right hand on his wounded leg and prayed. Within a few moments, the wound healed.

The mother hugged her son, looked up at Matthew, and kissed his hand. Matthew nodded as he stepped toward another bed. The nurse walked up to the doctor, anxious and tense.

"We're out of blood," said the nurse.

The doctor looked distressed and worried. Matthew turned to the doctor.

"I'm a universal blood type. Maybe I can help," said Matthew.

The doctor hesitated, then nodded. The nurse brought the apparatus and inserted the needle into Matthew's forearm. The tube overflowed with blood. The nurse quickly changed the tube, which overflowed too. Soon, the nurse filled up about a half dozen blood bags. Murmurs of doctors and nurses standing around could be heard. Matthew got dizzy for a moment, then reoriented himself shortly.

17 LOVE AND LEGACY

At the cottage, Analia sat at an old desktop computer, the hum of its aging machinery filling the room. She opened an electronic journal, its pages filled with detailed entries chronicling Matthew's extraordinary journey. Sophia entered the room, her eyes filled with curiosity as she observed her niece engrossed in her work.

"What're you working on, Ana?" asked Sophia.

"I'm chronicling Matthew's life, Aunt Sophia. It's all for my next book," replied Analia.

"Are you included in his journey?" Sophia teased.

Analia smiled, a tender warmth radiated from her as her gaze drifted toward the window.

"Are you going to wait for him all night?" asked Sophia.

"He'll be back soon," Analia replied.

Analia rose from her chair and made her way toward Matthew's farmhouse. She entered the house through the side door, stepping into the dimly lit living room. Sitting on the sofa, Davina brushed her long hair. Analia sat beside her.

"It worries me sick, Ana. He ventures into the war zones, risking his safety to heal others. He won't listen to me," said Davina.

Analia kept staring out the window. "He won't listen to any of us," said Analia.

Analia placed her arm around Davina, offering a moment of solace. Sebastian emerged from the kitchen.

"Our worry will not change the course he's destined to follow. We must have faith in his journey," said Sebastian.

Davina let out a deep sigh. The weight of her concerns was still evident on her face.

18 HOPE AMIDST CHAOS: CALL FOR TRANSFORMATION

One year later…

Matthew performed various community services around the country. He handed out relief to civil war victims in Los Angeles, fed the hungry in Chicago, healed the victims of natural disasters in Hawaii, and prayed with children and women huddled together in a homeless center in Milwaukee.

In San Francisco, surrounded by a small crowd, Matthew preached in a park littered with rubble and craters from shelling.

"My dear brothers and sisters, my weeping heart bleeds as I witness the pain and the suffering of our fellow beings," said Matthew.

The crowd grew larger as Matthew spoke, his face filled with love and compassion.

"The seeds of a worldwide revolution demanding change are forming. It's time to reform our planet for peace, justice, and equality for all," said Matthew. The crowd broke into applause and chants.

In an activist chapter in Miami, Matthew inspired a large crowd, gathered in excitement, chanting slogans.

"We must organize in every city of every nation on this planet. The world is on a path toward social, political, and ecological disaster. A radical transformation is inevitable," asserted Matthew. The activists murmured in agreement, some bowing their heads in reverence.

In Washington DC, a crowd of reporters listened intently, cameras flashing intermittently.

"The extremism of our isms and schisms has become a threat to the sustainability of the human race. It is time to take back our planet from the evil grips of the corrupt leaders and rulers…" Matthew said.

In Times Square, New York, amid towering skyscrapers and flashing neon lights, hundreds of people gathered, their eyes fixed on a colossal outdoor TV screen broadcasting the news. A News Anchor in her 40s addressed the camera.

"As endless wars and unrest tear the world apart, the man who disavows being the Second Coming hails a new, hopeful future," said the News Anchor.

The crowd erupted into excitement, cheering, and chanting.

19 ANALIA'S LITERARY OASIS: SIGNING DREAMS IN MY SOUL

San Diego, California.

Amid the chaos of the civil war, an old shopping mall stood defiantly. Broken windows and damaged walls bore witness to the chaos that surrounded it. The sound of intermittent shells from nearby cities echoed through the air. Devoted fans gathered for a book signing event, defying the constant danger that had become a part of their war-torn existence. The storefront was decorated with a large banner featuring the cover of Analia's novel Dreams in My Soul. Stacks of the book were neatly arranged around Analia.

The organizer, a poised woman in her late 40s, stepped forward, holding a microphone.

"It's an honor to present to you novelist Analia Garcia!" said the organizer.

The fans erupted into cheers and applause. Analia smiled graciously. She began signing books and engaging in short conversations with each fan. After signing several books, Analia took a moment to catch her breath.

"Thank you all for joining us. Let me share some excerpts from the book," said Analia.

She flipped open a copy of her novel and read an excerpt, "When the pain and passion converge, ideas spring from the realm of nowhere and everywhere."

The fans cheered as Analia signed a few more books. Amid the excitement, a fan stepped forward, holding her freshly signed copy.

"What's your next book about, Analia?" the fan asked. Analia's eyes lit up with enthusiasm.

"It'll be my first biographical novel based on the revolutionary journey of Matthew," Analia said.

The fans applauded, excited by the prospect of Analia's upcoming work. Another fan couldn't resist asking a more personal question.

"Analia, do you have a romantic relationship with Matthew?"

Analia's smile softened as she gazed out at her adoring fans.

"I love Matthew as millions of people do. His story deserves to be told," Analia replied.

The fans burst into cheers, applauding her enigmatic response. Analia signed a few more books. The line of people with wide-eyed excitement continued to snake through the store, eager to meet Analia and get their copy of the book signed.

20 UNBEARABLE BURDEN: DAVINA FEARS LOSING MATTHEW

Davina sat on the couch, Matthew sitting beside her. She turned to Matthew, her voice filled with worry and concern.

"I have a bad feeling about your rally in the midst of a civil war," said Davina.

Matthew reached out and took Davina's hand. He held it firmly, offering a sense of reassurance in his touch.

"Don't worry so much, Mother," said Matthew.

"But you are exposing yourself to danger every day. I won't be able to bear the pain if anything happens…" said Davina.

Matthew's expression became resolute.

"I'm organizing the masses for a revolution, Mother. There will be risks," Matthew said.

He wrapped his arm around Davina.

"I can't shake off my worries. The world outside is consumed by violence," said Davina.

Matthew gazed into Davina's eyes, his voice filled with empathy and understanding.

"I understand your fear, Mother, but I can't stand idle while humanity suffers," Matthew said. Davina's eyes welled up with tears as she held onto Matthew.

"Let us pray…" Davina said. She led a solemn prayer, tightly clasping Matthew's hand.

21 A PLAN FOR MATTHEW'S RALLY TAKES SHAPE

An SUV drove up to Matthew's farmhouse, kicking up a cloud of dirt. Russel, a forty-three-year-old former Special Forces commander with a rugged appearance and a military haircut, emerged from the vehicle. He wore a tactical vest and carried an army bag. Davina emerged from the interior and embraced Russell as Sebastian clapped him on the shoulder.

"Your aunt is worried sick about the big rally. We need your help to make sure everything goes smoothly," said Sebastian.

Davina took a deep breath, turning to Russell.

"We would feel so much safer if you could stay with us for a while," Davina said.

Russell nodded, accepting the responsibility placed upon him.

"I'll do everything to ensure Matthew's safety. First, we must scout the perimeter," said Russell.

Sebastian and Russell headed out toward the perimeter of the farmhouse. They methodically scanned the surroundings, their senses heightened. Russell led the way, inspecting trees, checking bushes, and scrutinizing fences.

22 MATTHEW RALLIES THE MASSES FOR A NEW WORLD ORDER

A large crowd gathered, defying the chaos that engulfed the cities, their faces filled with weariness and despair. Russell and an associate stood guard near the stage. Analia stepped up to the podium and took hold of the microphone.

"Ladies and gentlemen, humanity has waited long for this moment. The man who disclaims being the Second Coming, has come with a transformational vision for our world," said Analia.

The crowd erupted into rapturous applause and cheers, their weary faces lighting up with renewed hope. Matthew stepped onto the podium. He raised his hands, brought them to his heart, and bowed slightly, acknowledging the crowd's devotion. The crowd dropped silent, captivated by his presence. With his charismatic voice and mannerisms, Matthew delivered a spellbinding speech.

"As we stand together, here and now, humanity faces its darkest times. I call upon all to cease all acts of war, genocides, and terrorism that ravage our world," said Matthew.

The crowd listened intently, holding their banners and placards aloft, some read "Stop the tyranny" and "End the violence."

"It is time to build a borderless One World under God without the divisiveness and extremism of organized religion and organized politics," said Matthew.

A murmur of agreement rippled through the crowd, their faces filled with determination. Scores of television reporters transmitted Matthew's speech to viewers across the globe. Drones hovered above, capturing aerial footage of the momentous event. Massive outdoor television screens in Times Square and worldwide broadcast Matthew's speech live.

One of the screens displayed a breaking news headline: "Renowned Buddhist leader Disha Bakti declares Matthew as the incarnation of revered Buddhist prophet Maitreya."

Matthew continued his speech, "As foretold by prophets, ominous rulers have misled the world with false promises and flawed ideologies, staining this planet with greed, deceit, and moral decay."

Another breaking news headline read, "A coalition of prominent human rights organizations nominates Matthew for Nobel Peace Prize."

Matthew continued, "When our president incites separatist violence through hateful rhetoric for the sake of politics, it brings the nation to its knees, killing thousands and sending shockwaves across the country. It is time for President Williams to step down. We must end the civil war at home and our foreign wars now."

A surge of resolve washed over the crowd, their cries for change growing louder. Another screen displayed the breaking news headline: "Prominent scholar Arham Faisal proclaims Matthew as the reincarnation of Prophet Isa."

Matthew continued his captivating speech, "I call upon you in every corner of the globe to join the blazing revolution we have sparked for the transformation of our world. United as one, we will dismantle the walls of injustice, crush the flames of corruption, and pave the way for a new world to emerge. May God bless you, and may God bless our planet."

The crowd erupted in resounding applause and chants, their hope reignited by words of inspiration and revolution.

An elderly woman in the audience stepped forward.

"Are you the Second Coming of Christ we've been waiting

for?" asked the elderly woman.

Matthew paused, his gaze sweeping over the crowd.

"I'm only paving the way…" said Matthew.

A young woman in her 30s asked, "It seems you're trying to abolish all existing religions and create a new religion."

"What I envision is not a new religion, but a kingdom of heaven within us detached from the divisiveness of religions," replied Matthew.

A young man in his 20s standing across shouted out in anger. "Where's your God when the world's going to hell?"

The crowd around them became agitated, their voices rising in disagreement. Matthew raised his hand. The crowd fell into a reverent silence.

Matthew closed his eyes, a radiant light enveloping him. He began to levitate, gracefully floating toward the young man. Fear filled the young man's eyes as Matthew approached him. Instead of condemnation, Matthew embraced him, offering a moment of affirmation.

"May God be with you," said Matthew.

Awestruck for a moment, the crowd broke into roaring cheers, tears streaming down a few faces. Matthew walked among the crowd, some embracing him while others kissed his hand in admiration.

23 INTRIGUE AT THE WHITE HOUSE

Two security operatives in their 30s stood guard at the White House entrance, checking IDs and appointments. Colonel Cyrus Gideon (late 50s with a military haircut, arrogant and abrasive) approached.

"Do you have an appointment, Colonel?" asked a female guard.

Colonel Cyrus, visibly irritated, stared down at the guard with a piercing gaze.

"I don't need any damn appointment. Call the President," said Colonel Cyrus.

The security guards exchanged a concerned glance. The female guard called her superior through the earpiece.

"Sir, we have a Colonel Gideon here. He insists on seeing the President without an appointment," said the guard.

Indistinct conversations emanated from the earpiece as the guard received instructions. Colonel Cyrus reached into hidden holsters strapped to his waist and retrieved two handguns. He extended them toward the security guards.

"Hold on to these for me," Colonel Cyrus said.

The guards, momentarily taken aback, hesitated for a moment. Sensing the urgency, the male guard quickly scanned Colonel Cyrus with a handheld metal detector.

"He's good to go," said the male guard.

A White House staffer approached.

"I'll escort Colonel Gideon inside," the staffer said.

"About time…" Colonel Cyrus said sternly.

The guards exchanged puzzled glances as Colonel Cyrus followed the White House staffer.

24 DARK DECISION: COVERT ACTION

President Williams met with several leaders. He paced around, fuming with anger.

"I have enough problems on my hands. And now this radical cult figure is stirring up the masses," President Williams said.

The CIA Director, Gavin Miles, a calm and shrewd man in his early 50s, responded.

"Our intel shows Matthew is mobilizing tens of thousands of activists worldwide. His message is gaining traction, and he poses a significant threat to the current structure," Miles said.

"He's making the world question our authority, and he's making me look heinous. We need to squash his revolution before it gains more momentum," President Williams said.

"He's just a preacher, Sir. I'm not sure about the level of threat he poses. Targeting him could backfire and create a backlash," said Vice President Madison.

President Williams dismissed her concerns, driven by his desire to maintain power and control.

"We can't underestimate him. He's turning the masses against us, against our way of life. Revolutions always turn violent eventually. We can't let a religious extremist disrupt the global order," President Williams said.

The President of the National Evangelical Association, Noah Whitefield, a man in his late 60s, interjects.

"According to the prophecy of the Millennial Reign, he'll rule this world for a long time. But the problem is he wants to abolish organized religion. Our largest religions collect over a hundred billion dollars in tithe money from the public annually," Noah said.

"What do you suggest?" asked President Williams.

"Some extremist groups are planning to take him out. I'll reach out to Matthew and try to bring him to the mainstream," said Noah.

"Mr. President, I suggest a preemptive strike to neutralize the threat," Colonel Cyrus said.

"That's risky, Mr. President. If leaked, it would create a PR nightmare," said Vice President Madison.

President Williams unbuttoned his coat and stepped forward.

"He must be stopped if he plans to decimate the established structure," President Williams said.

"And if he can't be stopped?" asked NSA director Collin.

President Williams clenched his jaw.

"Then he must be eliminated. He's a threat to our power," President Williams said.

"His lunatic idea of redistribution of wealth must be discredited. I suggest we start by launching a disinformation campaign against Matthew and any foreign leaders collaborating with him," CIA director Miles said.

President Williams nodded.

"Who is funding his revolution?" asked President Williams.

"A disillusioned aviation tycoon named Elijah Moses," said NSA director Collin.

"We should surveil his office and anyone connected to Matthew. Meanwhile, let's work with our allies in Congress to get rid of the damn term limit. We also have to consider Martial Law," said President Williams.

"Yes, Mr. President," said Vice President Madison.

"I don't think a disinformation campaign will be enough," said President Williams.

"A covert strike can be arranged, Mr. President," Colonel Cyrus said.

President Williams looked at the directors of the CIA and NSA. The room fell silent as the words sank in. Both directors nodded. The Vice President remained uncommitted. President Williams stared at her, then turned to Col. Cyrus.

"You have my authorization," President Williams said.

"I think we should capture him alive," NSA Director Collin said.

"We'll do our best, Sir," said Colonel Cyrus.

"What if we let him destabilize the world?" asked CIA Director Miles.

"Then we can take him out and restore order afterward. We save the world and come out on top," President Williams said.

President Williams nodded as he paced, a cruel smile on his lips. The room hung heavily with silence as the weight of their decisions loomed overhead.

25 WEAPONIZING THE FUTURE

Later that night… At the CIA Headquarters.

"Sir, the CEO of Vision Defense is on the line," the Administrative Assistant said.

"Put him on the secure line," said CIA Director Miles. The Administrative Assistant patched the call.

"Good afternoon. What's new, my friend?" asked the CEO.

"The wars will help us get rid of the old weapons. We have to build next-generation weapons," said Miles.

"So, I can count on you to help us with the bid?" asked the CEO.

"You bet," said CIA Director Miles.

"Our team is already working on some groundbreaking weaponry," said the CEO.

"We need a revolutionary weapon system to counter the expansionism of Russia and China," said Miles.

"We can show you the prototypes within a month," the CEO said.

"I have to convince the government that your system is far superior to our other contractors," said Miles.

"I can assure you it's the future of defense. It's faster, more accurate, and more customizable than anything on the market," the CEO said.

"Alright, let's discuss the details when we meet," said Miles. Miles hung up the phone.

26 IN THE CROSSFIRE: SEBASTIAN'S BRAVE LAST MOMENTS

Sebastian opened the back of his pickup truck. Matthew came out of the barn and loaded crates of fresh produce onto the truck bed.

"Let me come with you, Dad," said Matthew.

"I'll be fine," Sebastian said.

"It's not safe for you to go out there anymore," said Matthew.

"I've been doing this for a long time, Son," Sebastian said.

Sebastian climbed into the truck and closed the door. He reached under the seat, retrieving a worn handgun, and tucked it discreetly behind his back. Matthew's worry intensified as he gazed at his father. Sebastian nodded before slowly driving away. Matthew stood there, watching the truck disappear into the distance, a mix of concern and uncertainty etched on his face.

Sebastian approached the old part of the city, which was filled with debris and burning vehicles littering the roadside. He turned on the radio news.

"The Southern separatist leader nicknamed "Darkangel Patriot" has called all nationalists to unite," said the reporter.

Several government military vehicles entered the highway from the back road, chasing Sebastian's truck. He swerved and ducked, crashing into a pile of rubble and toppled cars. He heard rumblings of throbbing explosions approaching his vehicle. As he looked into the rearview mirror, an RPG hit his truck. Metal screeched and glass shattered as the truck flipped several times, crashing down on its side.

Sebastian bled, lying upside down in the toppled truck, pain etched across his face. His trembling hand fumbled for his phone. He hit the speed-dial button.

"I need help...I'm hit..." Sebastian said into his phone.

"Oh God...no...no," Davina screamed.

Sebastian's vision blurred as he fought to keep his eyes open.

"Stay with me... we're on the way," Davina sobbed.

Sebastian's truck lay mangled in the middle of the road, its tires still spinning weakly. Smoke billowed from the wreckage. A separatist Humvee roared by his crashed vehicle, pursued by a government military truck. The vehicles exchanged gunfire, bullets whizzing in the air.

Through the shattered windshield, Sebastian glimpsed a government vehicle approaching. It sped toward him, closing the distance rapidly and slamming into his truck. The truck flew into the air, crashing and hitting the rocks below the hill. Sebastian lay motionless as silence descended upon the scene, broken only by the distant sounds of war and the chaos on the streets above.

27 THE CALLING RENEWS:
THE LIGHT OF REVELATION

Analia and Sophia slowly knelt to lay flowers on the freshly dug grave. Davina sobbed silently, sitting by the tiny grave of her infant daughter beside the new one. Matthew comforted her as tears rolled down her face.

"You were his pride and joy until the very end..." said Davina.

Matthew took a deep breath and exhaled sharply.

"I know he wanted you to follow your calling, though I always feared it," said Davina.

Matthew put his arm around his mother as she held him tightly.

"I think that ambush was meant for me," said Matthew. Davina's eyes widened with a mix of fear and sorrow.

"Don't blame yourself. I wish you would give up your mission. I don't want to lose you too..." said Davina.

Matthew sighed deeply, his gaze fixed on the casket before them, his eyes shimmering with tears. Sophia walked over and placed a comforting hand on Davina's shoulder. Analia stepped closer to Matthew, wrapping her arm around him.

Later that night...

Matthew prayed, sitting at the mouth of a cave on the low hill. The full moon shone brightly above him.

"Dear God, if I'm the one, show me the way as I struggle with my fear and doubt," said Matthew.

He closed his eyes and meditated for a long moment, his face reflecting his inner struggle. The crickets and the frogs sounded their mating songs as the wind howled.

Suddenly, a blinding light illuminated the night sky. A strong gust of wind forcefully pushed Matthew inside the cave. Awestruck in stunned fear, Matthew stumbled but quickly recovered. He ran outside, shielding his eyes from the intense light. A divine voice spoke to his mind. Matthew took hesitant steps back toward the cave. He knelt on the ground, his eyes cast downward.

"Follow your path, my child!" the divine voice said.

Matthew's voice trembled with conviction, his doubts slowly giving way to an inspired sense of purpose.

"My Lord, I will follow where you lead me," said Matthew.

Matthew sat there silently, with renewed determination. He bowed his head and prayed as the blinding light faded away.

28 A WORLD IN REVOLT

The news studio bustled with activity, with monitors displaying live feeds from various locations. A news anchor in her 40s addressed the studio camera.

"Following Matthew's call for President Williams' resignation, millions took to the streets to protest the civil war and the foreign wars," said the news anchor.

The footage captured vast crowds of protesters flooding the streets in major cities across the United States and around the globe. Holding signs that demanded peace and justice, their voices resonated through the air.

Some protesters clashed with heavily armed police officers. The sound of bullets and tear gas could be heard. Dozens of protesters were killed or wounded as clashes with the police intensified.

"A US Congressional Committee has launched an investigation into President Williams' role in inciting the Civil War. We will continue to monitor the situation and provide you with the latest updates as they unfold," said the news anchor.

29 THE MERCENARY'S HEART: WRECKER'S INTERNAL STRUGGLE

Wrecker, a forty-year-old imposing figure, tall and rugged, paced in the courtyard. He embodied a mysterious blend of a dedicated father and a mercenary assassin. His seven-year-old daughter, Angel, happily played on the swing while her loyal Labrador Retriever trailed behind her.

"Papa, can I ride the pony?" asked Angel. Wrecker looked at Angel, a tender smile crossing his face.

"Sure, sunshine," replied Wrecker.

Wrecker strode to the barn and returned, leading a gentle horse. He lifted Angel onto the horse and helped her settle in the saddle. Her face lit up with delight as the horse walked toward the backyard.

Suddenly, Wrecker's eyes caught sight of a dark limousine approaching the perimeter. Reacting swiftly, he pulled out a handgun from his back, positioning himself behind a tree. He aimed his gun at the approaching vehicle.

"That's close enough. Step out with your hands in the air," said Wrecker.

Colonel Cyrus complied with Wrecker's order, stepping out of the limousine.

"What're you doing here, Colonel?" asked Wrecker.

"I need a mercenary crew," replied Colonel Cyrus.

Colonel Cyrus lit a cigar, puffing on it before continuing.

"It'll be the biggest gig you ever had," said Colonel Cyrus.

Wrecker's gaze flickered toward Angel, playing innocently nearby. He sighed, torn between his responsibilities as a father and the dangerous world he had been a part of.

Col. Cyrus gazed at Wrecker's farm.

"Five mil can do wonders for someone starting over," said Colonel Cyrus.

Wrecker tucked his gun under his belt, considering the offer carefully.

"It costs a lot to put together a good crew these days," said Wrecker.

Col. Cyrus raised an eyebrow, intrigued by Wrecker's response.

"Are you negotiating?" asked Colonel Cyrus.

"I can do it for ten mil," replied Wrecker.

Col. Cyrus stepped back into his limousine, making a call. Indistinct conversations followed before he stepped out again, nodding in agreement.

"You've got a deal," Colonel Cyrus said.

Col. Cyrus drove off. Wrecker's expression turned conflicted as he watched it disappear into the distance.

He reached into his pocket and pulled out a hip flask, taking a long sip of alcohol. Shaking his head, he stood up and walked toward a private cemetery behind his farmhouse. He stopped before a grave adorned with a simple headstone. Angel's pony quietly approached, drawing near.

"Papa, I want to get down," Angel said.

Wrecker helped Angel off the pony. She stood beside him, both looking at the grave.

"Sometimes I can't remember her face, but I miss her anyway," Angel said.

Wrecker took a deep breath, his eyes filled with unspoken pain.

"Is she in Heaven, Papa?" asked Angel. Wrecker paused for a moment.

"There's no such thing sweetie. If there were a God, why would he take her away from you?" said Wrecker.

Angel looked at her father, her confusion and sadness evident. Wrecker pondered, consumed by his thoughts and the weight of his choices.

30 UNFULFILLED DREAMS: ANALIA LONGS FOR A NORMAL LIFE

Sitting underneath the shades of a tree, Matthew meditated as a flock of white doves surrounded him. Analia took a stroll along the beach. She reached the foot of the hill where Matthew meditated. Matthew opened his eyes and smiled as Analia sat beside him. He gently clasped her hand, drawing a deep breath.

"I must finish what I started before my time runs out," said Matthew.

Analia looked at Matthew with sadness on her face.

"I worry that your destiny will consume you," said Analia. Matthew gazed deeply into her eyes, then kissed her. Analia's eyes glistened with tears as she struggled with her emotions.

"What about our dreams of a simple life, of raising a family together? Will our dreams be sacrificed for the greater good? I don't know why you can't ever think of your own happiness," Analia said.

"How can I think of my happiness when the world is on the brink of an apocalypse?" Matthew asked.

"I know your path was chosen by God, but sometimes I wish for a different path," said Analia.

"The weight of my purpose may seem overwhelming at times, but you are what keeps me grounded in this chaotic world," said Matthew.

"I know your heart is burdened with the world's troubles,

but we too, deserve happiness, even in the face of darkness," Analia said.

Matthew sighed deeply. "God gave us free will to shape our destiny. But the corrupt will of the leaders has led us down the wrong path," Matthew said.

"It's always been like this. Most rulers have ruled by deception," Analia said.

"If the End Times prophecies are true, an Armageddon would decimate two-thirds of humanity. But there's still time to steer the world to a different path," said Matthew.

Matthew stood up and helped Analia to her feet, heading toward the farmhouse. Analia strolled silently with a sad expression in her eyes.

31 BUILDING A FORCE: RUSSELL'S PLAN TO PROTECT MATTHEW

Major Russell navigated through the city, eventually reaching a fortress concealed within the depths of the surrounding forest in Mount Shasta. As Russell approached the towering gate, the atmosphere turned tense. The security forces fired several warning shots around his SUV.

"Turn off your engine and step out with your hands behind your head," an unseen guard said in the megaphone.

Russell complied and remained composed.

"Approach the gate and state your name and purpose," the unseen guard said.

Russell took a few measured steps toward the gate, his gaze locked with the guard. A small metal window embedded in the side of the gate slid open. A security guard aimed his gun directly at Russell.

"Major Russell. I have urgent business with Captain Jackson," said Russell.

The security guard communicated with Captain Jackson through his earpiece.

"Major Russell to see you, Sir," the guard said.

"Bring him in," Jackson replied.

The guard led Russell to a sprawling field where dozens of young men and women were being trained - military style. The air was filled with the sounds of combat drills and the faint echoes of shouted commands. The commander of the training facility was Captain Jackson, a former Marine in his late 30s, eccentric and battle-scarred with a burning gaze. Jackson spotted Russell and approached him.

"What's new with you, Major? The big brothers got a hit on me," Jackson said.

Russell followed Jackson as they traversed the training ground.

"I bet they've got a hit on me too. What're you building here?" Russell asked.

"Private army for hire. The world's gone mad, Major," replied Jackson.

They reached a section where hand-to-hand combat training was taking place. Jackson signaled the trainer. The trainer was Summer Chen, a hardened and withdrawn former CIA operative in her early 30s. Three of them walked through various areas of the training ground.

"What brings you here, Major?" asked Summer.

Russell's expression softened as he looked at Summer, a mix of regret and longing in his eyes.

"I guess I was missing you," replied Russell.

"You gave up that right long ago," Summer said.

Russell's voice carried a tinge of remorse as he responded.

"You're blaming me for what happened?" Russell asked.

"You shouldn't have given up so easily," Summer replied.

"Classic case of displaced anger," Russell said.

Summer's eyes narrowed, her frustration evident.

"I'm burned. CIA's hunting for me," Summer said.

Jackson interjected, a sense of camaraderie in his voice.

"The system turned on us," said Jackson.

Russell nodded in agreement, a determination surfacing in his tone.

"We shouldn't have to accept the way it is," Russell said.

"This is all I know…" said Jackson.

"Then let's use it to safeguard someone who can change the world. I'm putting a team together to protect Matthew," Russell said.

"How do you know if he's real?" asked Jackson.

"Even if he's not the Second Coming, I think, as a revolutionary figure, he'll change the world," Russell replied. Jackson glanced at Summer, seeking her response.

"Is the system after him?" Summer asked.

Russell solemnly nodded. Summer's voice carried a newfound resolve.

"I'm in, all the way," said Summer.

Jackson paced a bit, considering the idea, and then signaled one of his associates. A man in his late 20s approached him.

"Get the crew ready," Jackson said.

32 DOUBLE THREAT: RUSSELL REVEALS BOUNTIES ON MATTHEW

Matthew and his followers gathered for Thanksgiving dinner. Matthew clasped his hands together, leading the prayer.

"… on this Thanksgiving Day, fill our hearts with compassion and humility, and stir us to service to humanity…" said Matthew.

Everyone bowed their heads in reverence, then began serving themselves, passing dishes around with gratitude. Matthew stared at his plate, exhaling sharply.

"Every time I sit down to have a meal, my heart aches for the millions who starve. Every time I lie down on my bed, my soul bleeds for billions who suffer in the sweltering slums…" Matthew said.

A solemn silence descended upon the room as Matthew's words sank in.

"I would like to collaborate with the United Nations to set up some humanitarian centers around the world," said Matthew.

Elijah Moses, an older follower in his late 60s with thick glasses, coughed and cleared his throat before responding.

"We'll try to set up a meeting with the Secretary-General. I hope the UN will welcome our willingness to collaborate," said Elijah.

Russell turned to Matthew. "Matthew, for security reasons, we should move into our trailer base," said Russell.

Lee Anand, an idealistic follower in his early 30s, adjusted his heavy-rimmed glasses.

"With Brother Elijah's support, our base is ready. We have our own power supply, communication system, and other vital resources," Lee said.

Russell's phone buzzed with incoming messages. He quickly checked them, his expression turning serious.

"Sorry to interrupt. There are two bounties on you, Matthew - one by the religious extremists and the other by the government," Russell said.

"Only two? I must be losing my touch," Matthew said. Laughter filled the room as the tension eased momentarily.

33 EYES ON THE FARMHOUSE

A high-tech surveillance room with multiple large screens displayed live video feeds of Matthew's farmhouse. Several male and female operatives in their 20s and 30s sat at their stations, reviewing the feeds with intense focus. Col. Cyrus stood at the center, monitoring the situation. Major Russell's image and data appeared on the screen. Col. Cyrus stared at it, a flicker of recognition crossing his face.

"I served with him. We can't underestimate him," said Colonel Cyrus.

Col. Cyrus swiftly moved his attention to the facial recognition analysis of each follower on the monitor.

"Hold it there! Zoom in!" said Colonel Cyrus.

The screen froze, revealing the images of Jackson and Summer. Col. Cyrus studied their faces with a mix of concern and respect.

"We've got a formidable enemy here. We must reinforce our crew," said Colonel Cyrus.

He reached into his pocket and retrieved his phone. A determined look settled on his face as he dialed a number.

34 THE DEN OF RESISTANCE: THE HIDDEN TRAILER BASE

Behind Matthew's farmhouse, hidden amid the dense woods, stood a trailer. Adjacent to it, a helicopter rested on the ground. Matthew and his followers gathered in the trailer and watched the breaking news on a wall-mounted monitor.

"I implore everyone not to be deceived by this false prophet whose stunts and illusions are radicalizing countless youths, luring them into a dangerous cult revolution that threatens to destabilize our entire world," President Williams said. Matthew smiled, a melancholy but serene expression on his face.

"That maniac powermonger has to go. His secret squads have been targeting our student activists for years," said Lee.

"As always, he's resorting to deception and disinformation," said Summer.

"Son of a bitch is an evil fascist. News reports show he has connections to Neo-Nazi groups," Jackson said.

"The corrupt will always try to tarnish the image of those who challenge their power. We must not let his lies distract us from our purpose. We need to join forces with conscientious leaders within and beyond our borders," Matthew said.

"We'll set up confidential meetings with the leaders who share our cause," said Elijah.

"We can create a united front against President Williams' tyranny. Together, we can bring down his corrupt regime," said Matthew.

Matthew's followers nodded in agreement, their determination growing stronger. Russell exited, concern and worry etched on his face. Summer and Jackson followed him closely behind. In the courtyard, Russell, Summer, and Jackson discussed security issues with a half-dozen operatives.

"Alright, split up and take positions around the perimeter. We can't afford any surprises. Stay alert and report anything suspicious immediately," Russell said.

The operatives nodded, acknowledging their orders, and began to patrol the perimeters.

Jackson lit a cigarette and then turned to Russell.

"What made you quit the Forces, Major?" asked Jackson.

Russell took a moment to gather his thoughts, his eyes reflecting a mix of frustration and resignation.

"I suppose it's the same story - endless wars for the glory of our leaders," replied Russell.

Jackson nodded, acknowledging Russell's sentiment.

"Different times, different leaders - same fucking story," said Jackson. Jackson's gaze shifted to Summer.

"What's your story with the CIA? What sorts of gigs did you have?" asked Jackson.

Summer paused, staring into the distance as she recalled her past.

"From wetwork to weapons delivery - I've done it all. I've seen the darkest corners of humanity," replied Summer.

Russell reached into his pocket, retrieving a hip flask. He took a long sip of alcohol, his face contorted in a mixture of pain and regret. Summer's worry-filled eyes locked with Russell's, her voice tinged with concern.

"I thought you quit," said Summer.

Russell's expression softened with a bitter smile.

"Try dealing with my shell shock. It haunts me every damn day. If it weren't for Matthew, we'd still be selling our souls to the devils!" Russell said.

35 AMBUSH AT THE FARMHOUSE: MERCENARIES ATTACK

Three dark vans approached the far edges of the north perimeter, stopping behind a hill. Wrecker and a dozen black-clad mercenaries in full body armor jumped out of the vans with automatic weapons and rocket launchers.

Wrecker crept up behind Russell's security operative. They engaged in hand-to-hand combat. Wrecker fired his silenced gun, wounding the operative. The operative fell to the ground, barely conscious. He mustered the strength to reach for his earpiece. But before he could relay a distress call, Wrecker lunged forward, throwing the earpiece away. A thud echoed as Wrecker struck the operative's face with his submachine gun, rendering him unconscious.

At the south end of the perimeter, Wrecker's soldier zeroed in on Russell's operative. With calculated precision, he aimed and fired his silenced gun. The operative crumpled to the ground. Wrecker and his crew approached the farmhouse. As they got closer to the courtyard, they fired their weapons.

Russell barked into his earpiece, his voice laced with urgency. "Code Red! Code Red! Evac Matthew!"

Russell and his operatives frantically returned fire with submachine guns. Shouting and indistinct instructions can be heard amid the explosions. The followers exited the trailer and escorted Matthew toward the barn. An enemy rocket hit the farmhouse setting it ablaze. Searing blasts, fiery flashes, and clouds of ashes everywhere. Matthew, Analia, and Lee desperately made their way through the chaos toward the burning farmhouse, searching for Davina and Sophia. The heat of the flames intensified as they approached.

"Take Matthew to the cellar," Russell shouted into the earpiece.

Matthew, Analia, and Lee entered the burning farmhouse, the crackling flames and billowing smoke surrounding them. Debris and ash covered the floor, making it difficult to navigate.

"Aunt Sophia!" Analia screamed.

Matthew and Lee crawled through the wreckage, their eyes stinging from the smoke. They spotted the bodies of Davina and Sophia lying on the floor beneath the rubble. Analia let out a heart-wrenching scream, her grief consuming her. Matthew's eyes welled up with tears as he fell to his knees beside Davina and Sophia.

"God… no…" Matthew shouted.

"We need to get them out of here, Matthew," Lee said.

Matthew and Lee lifted Davina and Sophia, carrying them out of the burning house. Analia followed close behind, her cries echoing through the devastation. As they approached the barn, Wrecker, still in the distance, spotted them and quickly aimed with an RPG launcher. He fired, the rocket soaring through the air. The RPG hit near the barn, causing a massive explosion.

Inside the barn, Elijah lifted a hardwood door on the floor, revealing the narrow stairs to the storm cellar. Matthew and Lee hurriedly carried Davina and Sophia into the cellar. They laid them gently on the floor. Analia sobbed, her anguish overwhelming.

Matthew knelt beside his mother's wounded body. He placed his right hand on her wound, and his left hand on Sophia's injury. His eyes closed as he prayed, pouring his will into their healing. Slowly, the wounds healed, but Davina and Sophia remained unconscious. Analia, filled with despair

69

and fear, rested her head on Sophia's chest and sobbed.

Lee knelt beside them and checked their pulse.

"Their pulses are weak but steady," said Lee.

Within a few moments, Sophia regained consciousness. Analia lifted her head, hugging Sophia tightly, tears streaming down her face. Matthew held his mother's unconscious body, placing his trembling hand on her head. Within seconds, a faint movement stirred within Davina, her breathing shallow and labored.

Her eyes flickered open for a fleeting moment, filled with sadness. She looked at Matthew and tried to mouth some words, but her weakened state only allowed for a faint whisper.

"Matthew... my son..." said Davina.

Matthew lifted his mother's head gently in his arms.

"Mother, I'm here," Matthew said.

Davina brought her trembling lips to Matthew's forehead, leaving a final kiss. Her breathing grew shallower, and she took her final breath with one last sigh.

"No... Mother...no," Mathew screamed.

He held onto his mother's lifeless body tightly against his chest. He sat in silence staring at her serene face, feeling a deep sense of emptiness.

36 A LEADER FALLS: WRECKER'S MERCENARIES SEIZE MATTHEW

The intense gunfight continued to rage around the farmhouse. Rockets and bullets hit the gas furnace, exploding in a ball of flame.

"Take position in the ark! Move! Move!" Russell shouted into the earpiece.

Crawling through the thick smoke and debris, Russell and his operatives made their way to the nearby beach. They dived into the water, swimming toward the abandoned ship off the shore. Within seconds, several enemy rockets hit the ship, setting it ablaze. One of the operatives was wounded, bleeding heavily from his leg. Russell swiftly took off his outer shirt, tightly tying it around the wounded leg.

"You'll be alright, buddy. Hang in there," said Russell.

As the fire raged around the ship, Wrecker, followed by a combatant, stormed in. Summer engaged them in deadly hand-to-hand combat. In a fury of punches and spinning kicks, she knocked out Wrecker's soldier. Summer and Wrecker found themselves locked in a dangerous standoff, pointing their guns at each other. They simultaneously fired, but Summer quickly ducked and spun, firing again and hitting Wrecker's hand. His gun dropped out of reach.

Wrecker, forced into retreat, launched himself into the water. Summer relentlessly fired shots into the water, narrowly missing him. Wrecker dived deep and swam toward the beach, signaling two soldiers who sustained minor injuries. One of them handed Wrecker a submachine gun as they followed him.

Wrecker and his troops put on gas masks and silently approached the barn. They fired on the cellar door hinges, opening it. Lee, in a desperate attempt to defend the group, fired back. Wrecker ducked and tossed a gas canister into the cellar. Everyone succumbed to the choking gas, dropping to the floor in a coughing fit. Wrecker and his soldiers jumped into the cellar, firing at Lee, and injuring him.

Startled and horrified, everyone screamed as Wrecker hit Matthew's head with his submachine gun. Matthew blacked out, blood streaming from his wound. Analia's scream pierced the air. Wrecker and his troops seized Matthew's unconscious body and exited the cellar.

Wrecker and his soldiers hastily laid Matthew in the back of a van behind the hill, securing him with zip-cuffs and covering his head with a dark mask. Wrecker's remaining soldiers retreated from the courtyard, jumping into their vans. The three shadowy vans drove off.

Russell and his team fired multiple shots toward the vans. They're out of range. The vans disappeared into the darkness. The fire raged as Russell and his troops dived through the flames, plunging into the water. They swam back to the beach, some sustaining minor injuries. Russell rushed to the barn and looked down into the cellar. As Analia wept, everyone climbed out.

"They got Matthew," Lee said

"No… Goddamn it," said Russell.

"He's got a chip, we can track him," said Lee.

Lee swiftly checked his smartphone, tracing the tracking signal.

37 DIVINE INTERVENTION: MATTHEW ESCAPES

Matthew lay naked, curled up in the corner of a dark and freezing cell. Footsteps stopped outside the door. Colonel Cyrus and two operatives entered. One operative flipped a switch outside the door and turned on a dim light. Colonel Cyrus stood next to Matthew, looking stern. Matthew opened his eyes, disoriented and unsettled.

"Which world leaders are collaborating with you?" asked Colonel Cyrus.

Matthew's body shivered on the cold, dusty floor as he remained silent.

"I'll ask you one last time before these guys get to work," said Colonel Cyrus.

The operatives prepared for waterboarding with electric shock.

"Who are your collaborators?" asked Colonel Cyrus.

Matthew closed his eyes, taking a deep breath. The operatives moved forward and began the torture. Matthew gasped for air, pain etched on his face.

"Let's see how long you can hold up," Colonel Cyrus said. Matthew's screams filled the air, his body twisting in agony. Colonel Cyrus' phone rang, interrupting the torture. He answered, frustration in his voice.

"Yes, Sir," said Colonel Cyrus.

Colonel Cyrus threw Matthew's robe at him, and one of the operatives roughly put it on him.

"I've never seen a president come down to the dungeon," Colonel Cyrus smirked.

Within moments, President Williams entered the cell, accompanied by the directors of the NSA and CIA. Matthew stared at them in dismay and disbelief. NSA Director Collin took a step forward, skepticism in his voice.

"If you are a prophet, convince us right here with your powers," Collin said.

Matthew closed his eyes and silently prayed.

"It is not I who chooses when to use my power," said Matthew.

"Tell us how your power works," asked CIA director Miles.

"Everything cannot be explained by the depth of science you possess today," Matthew replied.

"If you have supernatural powers, then you must know what lies ahead," President Williams said.

Matthew remained silent. President Williams grew impatient.

"I'm sorry to say these guys enjoy doing what they do," President Williams said. The operatives exchanged glances.

"Sadly, humanity has not learned from history. One man can drive the world to the brink of collapse," Matthew said.

"You're causing chaos and anarchy. I'm doing what's in the best interest of this country," said President Williams.

"Is inciting hateful divisiveness and violence in our best interest? The civil war's tearing the nation apart, and your oil wars are killing millions overseas," said Matthew.

"What have you done lately other than spread your misguided ideas?" asked President Williams.

"I'm trying to undo what you have done, Mr. President. All you have done is for the sake of clinging to power," replied Matthew.

"Do you know how many snakes are in the grass, conspiring against me? Some of them would probably kill me if they could," said President Williams.

Matthew's gaze fell on the handguns holstered at President Williams' side.

"If a president acts like a despotic king and fears for his life in his own house, what good is it if he rules the world?" asked Matthew.

The operatives continued waterboarding with electric shocks.

"This can continue indefinitely. Tell us which UN leaders are with you," asked President Williams.

Matthew gasped for air, his voice strained but defiant.

"Is a global structure on a self-destructive path worth saving?" asked Matthew.

"I cannot allow you to take your restructuring Plan to the UN," said President Williams.

Matthew's voice remained calm. "You can hurt my body, but you can't harm my soul. The world will know," Matthew said.

Colonel Cyrus stepped forward, his voice filled with derision.

"You'll never get out of here. You're just another fake prophet," said Col. Cyrus. He signaled the operatives, who intensified the electric shocks.

Matthew struggled for breath, his agonized screams piercing the night. His breaths grew shallower and with one last tremor, his body became still. The room fell into a deep silence, the weight of the moment hanging heavily in the air. NSA Director Collin broke the silence.

"Damn it… you killed him."

Suddenly, the entire room went pitch black. Automated security systems sounded repeated voice warnings.

"Security breach. Evacuate," said the security alert.

Matthew slowly rose to his feet. He walked out of the dungeon, levitating toward the exit. He hovered in mid-air, bathed in a divine aura.

Russell tracked Matthew's location from the helicopter.

"How the hell are we gonna get in there?" asked Summer.

"Let's hope for a miracle," replied Jackson.

The pilot glanced at the scores of buttons in the cockpit. He pressed several buttons activating noise reduction, radar, and infrared detection mechanisms.

Matthew levitated higher, suspended above the courtyard. He stretched out his arms. The glow intensified around him as he ascended into the night sky. He looked up and spotted the chopper approaching. The divine radiance spread around him, enveloping the entire courtyard.

Two government operatives emerged from the shadows, running with their guns drawn. The first operative, stunned by the spectacle unfolding before him, was deeply moved.

"Dear Lord… he's the real one," said the first government operative.

He lowered his gun. The second operative remained resolute, his gun still aimed at Matthew.

"What the fuck is the matter with you?" exclaimed the first government operative.

The second operative's gaze remained fixed on the blinding light emanating from Matthew. He hesitated, torn between his duty and the inexplicable power he witnessed. The first operative placed his hand over the second operative's gun, gently pushing it down.

"This is something greater than us," said the first operative.

The second operative's eyes darted between Matthew and his colleague. Slowly, he lowered his gun, his face mirroring a mix of uncertainty and awe.

Russell spotted Matthew from above. He directed the pilot's attention to Matthew floating in mid-air. The pilot maneuvered the chopper closer to Matthew's location, hovering just above the courtyard. Matthew floated toward the open chopper door. Russell reached out and grabbed Matthew, his hands firmly clasping him. Summer joined

Russell, pulling Matthew safely into the helicopter's interior.

Three additional government operatives burst onto the scene, their weapons blazing as they unleashed a barrage of gunfire at the helicopter. Bullets rained down on the chopper, striking its structure.

The helicopter shuddered, struggling to maintain stability as part of it caught fire. The cabin shook violently, the wind whipping, warning lights flashing. Despite the flames spreading at the side of the chopper, the pilot managed to stabilize it and began searching for a suitable landing spot.

"Hang on! We gotta land it somewhere safe!" the pilot shouted over the noise.

Russell scanned the horizon as the chopper lurched through the air, smoke billowing from its engine.

"There! I see a clearing ahead," Russell said.

The chopper descended, struggling to maintain stability. Finally, it touched down with a violent jolt, skidding across the ground. Matthew and Jackson sustained minor head injuries.

"Everyone evacuate! Move! Move!" said Russell.

Russell and Summer helped Matthew descend, leading him away from the blazing chopper.

38 FAITH TESTED: ANALIA'S DOUBT

Despite the ravages of fire, the skeletal remains of the farmhouse defiantly endured. The trailer stood unscathed, its presence undeterred. A half-dozen male and female security operatives stood guard. Matthew sat hunched behind the trailer, his gaze drowned in sadness. Holding his arm tenderly, Analia sat beside him.

"They won't stop until they kill you," said Analia.

Matthew gazed into Analia's eyes, seeing the fear and anguish reflected in her expression.

"I can't stop now. Can I stand by and let tyranny prevail?" said Matthew.

Analia's voice quivered with doubt. "I'm losing my faith. Why didn't God let you save your mother?" asked Analia.

"My gift was overpowered by her soul as she didn't wish to return to earth," replied Matthew. He remained silent for a long moment.

"Too many people are dying. It's not what I envisioned," Matthew said.

"Then let's stop this and live a normal life. You can't start a worldwide revolution without consequences. The power elite won't allow it," said Analia.

"If you believe I was sent here to build lasting peace, how can I give up now? I can't stand idly by while humanity tears itself apart," Matthew said.

Overwhelmed with emotion, Analia's voice trembled.

"Countless revolutions throughout human history have brought chaos and casualties. Innocent lives were lost, and families were torn apart. What if you fail? Do you wish to die a martyr? Do you want to leave me behind alone?" Analia asked.

"I know I can't assure you of a painless path. You're not safe around me. This isn't a life for you," Matthew replied.

"I never thought my life was separate from yours," Analia said.

Matthew stared at Analia and paused. "I'll embark on a period of fasting and meditation. I need some time of prayer and solitude, away from distractions," said Matthew.

Analia rose, her voice filled with hurt and anger.

"Do whatever the hell you want," said Analia.

Matthew's gaze followed her, filled with a deep sense of sorrow and empathy.

39 A MISSING BEACON: THE WORLD AWAITS MATTHEW'S RETURN

Matthew wandered through the dense forest, far from the trailer, walking amid towering trees, contemplating, praying, and meditating.

At a television network, a news anchor in her 40s, addressed the studio camera.

"It's been weeks since the enigmatic figure known as Matthew, who captured the world's attention with his divine powers and mission, has been seen in public. There has been no official update from Matthew's team concerning his condition or whereabouts," said the news anchor. On a large screen behind the anchor, images of Matthew's previous appearances were displayed, highlighting his impact on the world.

"The absence of Matthew, during these trying times, has left the world at large with an overwhelming sense of concern," continued the news anchor.

The screen shows footage of people gathered in public spaces, discussing and speculating about Matthew's absence.

A chopper navigated above the dense and shadowy forest. The sunlight struggled to penetrate the thick foliage. Russell and Analia peered out, their eyes scanning the surroundings, searching for any sign of Matthew. Russell gripped his binoculars tightly as he scanned the landscape below.

"No sign of him." said Russell.

Analia's face reflected her deep concern as she looked around, hoping to catch even the faintest glimpse of Matthew.

"He may be in danger…" Analia said.

The chopper slowly maneuvered through the dense shrubs.

40 DESPERATE SEARCH FOR MATTHEW

Matthew lay asleep on the ground, tossing and turning. The gentle glow of moonlight poured through the trees. In his dream, he found himself lying on the deck of a grand mansion. He bled profusely from bullet wounds. Kneeling beside him, Analia cradled his head in her lap.

Matthew's vision shifted, and he saw his parents standing at the end of a dazzling light. They raised their hands toward him. He ran towards them, but they faded away. His eight-year-old self came into view, with Analia calling out to him, running after him.

Matthew saw his parents again, standing in front of the divine light. His face lit up with a sense of bliss and disbelief as he reached his parents. They embraced him tightly, tears of joy streaming down their faces. But as the moment unfolded, Matthew's parents began to fade away again, blending into the dissolving light.

Matthew found himself back on the deck of the mansion. Analia still held his head in her lap, her sobs echoing in the air.

"Let me go, Ana…" said Matthew.

The chopper's blades sliced through the air as it hovered over the sprawling forest.

"We have to find him and take him away from all this…" said Analia.

"He won't listen," said Russell.

"You're too compliant," Analia said.

"Can we defy a prophet?" asked Russell.

Russell looked through his binoculars. A break in the trees revealed a campfire. He handed the binoculars to Analia.

"It's him…" Analia said tensely.

"Take it down," Russell asked the pilot.

The chopper descended, maneuvering through the tangled branches and landing near the campfire. Matthew lay there, barely conscious of dehydration and malnourishment. Analia ran to Matthew, her anger melted away, and her anguish dissipated, replaced by relief and affection. She cradled his head in her lap, her voice trembling.

"I'm so sorry, Matthew. Please, forgive me," said Analia.

Matthew's eyes fluttered open, his breathing shallow. His gaze met Analia's tearful eyes, and a kind smile formed on his lips.

41 A SAFE HAVEN

A cozy cabin nestled deep within the woods by a glistening lake. Summer and two operatives patrolled the perimeter. The flames flickered from an old fireplace, casting a graceful glow in the room. Matthew awakened and looked around him.

"Where am I?" asked Matthew.

Analia put her arm around him, offering comfort and support. "We'll be safe here, you need to rest and recover fully," Analia said.

Matthew struggled to stand up. "I understand the danger of my purpose and the burden it places on those around me," said Matthew.

Analia's concern deepened as she helped him sit back on the bed.

"You're too weak, Matthew. You have to regain your strength. This cabin offers the security we need," Analia said.

"They will soon target those closest to me, Ana. It's safer if you stay here, hidden away. But I must return to our base," Matthew responded.

Analia reached out, her hand grasping Matthew's. Her face reflected a deep sadness at the thought of being separated.

"No, Matthew, I should stay by your side, even if it means facing the risks together," Analia said.

Matthew's eyes softened, his grip tightening around Analia's hand.

42 THE PRESIDENT'S RESOLVE: QUELLING THE GLOBAL UPRISING

President Williams sat behind his desk, frustration evident on his face. He watched the wall screen displaying news reports about Matthew's disappearance.

"Where is he hiding?" asked President Williams.

"We're doing everything we can to trace his whereabouts, Mr. President," said Colonel Cyrus.

"We underestimated his powers and his team. They are proving to be formidable obstacles," said NSA Director Collin.

"Major Russell is fiercely loyal to Matthew and will stop at nothing to protect him," said Colonel Cyrus.

"Why did he turn against us?" asked President Williams.

"He grew a conscience, Mr. President," replied NSA Director Collin.

President Williams looked at the TV screen, displaying news footage of massive rallies around the world, where activists called for the overthrow of corrupt leaders.

"The revolution is spreading like wildfire. We must take decisive action," said President Williams.

General Garrison, a towering figure in his early 60s, leaned forward and interjected.

"Do we need a backup crew, Colonel? This situation requires swift action," asked General Garrison.

"I assure you, General, I'll take him down," replied Colonel

Cyrus. President Williams nodded, determination shining in his eyes.

"Do whatever it takes, Colonel. Neutralize him and quell this uprising," said President Williams.

Colonel Cyrus saluted, acknowledging his orders, and exited the office.

43 ANALIA VOWS TO STAND BY MATTHEW'S SIDE

Analia and Matthew strolled hand in hand along the shore, their eyes reflecting love and affection. They rowed a boat in the moonlight, gliding smoothly across the serene lake. They dove into the crystal-clear water, gracefully moving through the surface, twirling and floating. As midnight approached, they found comfort in each other's arms, sitting on the porch. Analia leaned her head on his shoulder as Matthew kissed her.

"I'm crushed between my passion for you and the yearning for my calling," whispered Matthew.

"If they crucify you, I will rather go with you," Analia said.

Matthew lovingly wrapped his arm around Analia, drawing her closer.

"Your time is not now. I would rather have a life with you here than wait for you up there," said Matthew.

"I hope our fate can be altered," Analia said.

"The actions we take today can reshape our future. The prophecies are grounded on one version of the future," Matthew said.

"Can't we escape to a place unburdened by the world's weight on your shoulders?" asked Analia.

"After my mother died, I questioned everything. I yearned for another way. But deep down, I know my purpose extends beyond our earthly passion," replied Matthew.

"There's always a way if we're willing to accept it. We can find a path that blends our love and purpose," Analia said.

Analia's phone rang, breaking their intimate moment. She

put it on speaker mode, and Russell's urgent voice filled the air.

"The President has escalated the foreign wars, and he's instigating an ethnic-cleansing war at home," said Russel.

Matthew's expression turned resolute as he realized the urgency of the situation.

"I'll be on my way. He needs to be removed from power," said Matthew.

Analia hung up the call. Matthew gazed at Analia's disheartened face and put his arm around her.

"I'm so sorry, I must go," said Matthew.

"I can't let you go anywhere alone," said Analia.

Matthew stared at Analia's face, determination reflected in her eyes. He rose from the porch, reaching out and softly holding her hand.

44 MATTHEW REEMERGES WITH RENEWED DETERMINATION

Matthew entered his trailer base, looking weary and melancholy. His followers' faces bore expressions of concern and anguish. Elijah embraced him affectionately.

"I hope you won't disappear like that again," said Elijah.

"Please forgive me. I'm deeply troubled by the escalating wars, it tears at my heart," said Matthew.

"President Williams won't change his evil ways," said Lee.

"Matthew, we've received word that the UN Secretary-General is willing to meet with you. Should I arrange the meeting?" asked Elijah.

"Can we invite him to join us on our rally train?" asked Matthew.

Elijah nodded as he read a message on his phone.

"The president of the largest evangelical association wants to have a discrete meeting with you," Elijah said.

"This could be a setup," Jackson said.

"Can he too join us on the train? At least it's on our turf," said Matthew.

Russell stepped forward with a furrowed brow, hesitating for a moment.

"Matthew, the train trip poses significant risks," Russell said.

Matthew placed a hand on Russell's shoulder, acknowledging his concern.

"I understand your worries, Brother. We must forge ahead, even if the path is treacherous. It's unlikely that they would attack us while news choppers hover above, tracking our every move," Matthew said.

Russell stared at Matthew's resolute face, then turned to Elijah.

"We must ensure our choppers are upgraded for maximum defensive and offensive capabilities," Russell said.

Elijah nodded, his expression reflecting resolve.

"Matthew, a confidential source claims to have a secret audio recording from the White House, revealing the President's approval of the hit on you. Should we expose this to the media?" asked Elijah.

Matthew paused, then nodded.

45 ELIJAH UPGRADES CHOPPERS FOR MATTHEW'S SAFETY

The signage on the door read, "AeroSafe Aviation." A large floor-to-ceiling window overlooked a sprawling cityscape. Elijah sat at his desk, his eyes fixed on the manager, a man in his late 40s, seated across from him.

"We have to integrate the stealth defense urgently," said Elijah.

"How urgent, Sir?" asked the Manager.

"Two weeks max," Elijah replied.

"It'll be a significant technical challenge, Sir. We'll need an expanded task force," the Manager said.

"You will have all the resources you need," Elijah replied.

The telephone rang, interrupting their discussion.

"Sir, Major Russell on the line," the Admin Assistant said.

"Yes, Major," Elijah answered.

"We'll need two birds with stealth," Russell said.

"We can get one bird ready in two weeks," Elijah said.

"We don't have two weeks. Can we do it in one?" Russell asked.

"We'll do our best," Elijah replied. He hung up the phone and turned his attention back to the Manager.

"We'll need cutting-edge materials and design modifications with electronic countermeasures," the Manager said.

"We've always pushed the boundaries. I have faith in your team's expertise," Elijah said.

The Manager nodded in agreement, a sense of determination on his face.

46 ASSASSINATION PLOT EXPOSED

The newsroom pulsed with energy as journalists typed away on their keyboards. Paul Wilson, a seasoned news editor in his early 50s, sat at his desk with a phone pressed against his ear.

"What's new, Brother Elijah?" asked Paul.

"I'm in contact with a confidential source who claims to have a secret audio recording from the White House," Elijah replied.

"If you think it's credible, I need to hear it," said Paul.

"You'll hear from him shortly," Elijah said.

Paul ended the call. Within seconds, his phone rang. He took notes as he spoke with the confidential source.

"I'm sending the encrypted audio file," the confidential source said.

Paul quickly scanned his computer screen, searching for the incoming file, and gestured to his Tech Specialist, a young woman in her twenties.

"Let's run a voice analysis on it," said Paul.

The Tech Specialist swiftly acted, initiating the analysis on her computer while the chilling audio began to play.

"Then he must be eliminated. He's a threat to our power," President Williams said.

"A covert strike can be arranged, Mr. President," replied Colonel Cyrus.

"You have my authorization," said President Williams.

The Tech Specialist's eyes widened as she verified the

authenticity of the voice through her analysis.

"It's authentic, definitely the President's voice," said the Tech Specialist.

"It's explosive, damning," Paul said.

Paul hung up the phone and called the Assistant Editor on the intercom. The Assistant Editor, a woman in her 30s, entered the office.

"What's going on? You seem agitated," said the Assistant Editor.

"It's earth-shattering. We must break this story now. The President has authorized the assassination of Matthew," said Paul.

The Assistant Editor listened to the shocking audio clip. Her eyes welled up with shock and dismay.

"We should consult our legal team, protect the source, and expose the truth to the world," said the Assistant Editor.

"We can't waste a moment. Assemble the legal team," Paul said.

The Assistant Editor nodded, rushing toward her office.

47 WHITE HOUSE SCRAMBLES FOR DAMAGE CONTROL

President Williams, seething with anger and desperation, paced back and forth in his office. A large screen mounted on the wall broadcast the breaking news. A news anchor in her 40s reported.

"In a stunning revelation, an audio recording has surfaced, allegedly exposing the President's direct involvement in ordering a secret assassination of Matthew."

The footage showed the media worldwide reporting, sending shockwaves as audiences watched the news in horror. The President's face contorted with fury as he listened to the damning evidence against him.

"Who's the traitor? Who leaked the goddamn audio?" President Williams shouted.

"Mr. President, we're still investigating the source of the leak. It could be someone within our administration or an external party with insider knowledge," replied NSA Director Collin.

"Do we have deniability? Can we distance ourselves from this?" asked President Williams.

"The voice analysis technology is very accurate these days, Mr. President," said CIA Director Miles.

"I don't see any option for deniability, Sir," NSA Director Collin said.

"I want a special team to work on all possible damage control strategies. I'll not allow everything we've achieved to crumble. If we let him live, he'll take us down. We must eliminate this threat now, and we can use deniability, claiming the audio is AI generated," said President Williams.

"It's too risky to go down the same path, Mr. President. The public's trust is already waning, and manipulating the truth further may have dire consequences," NSA Director Collin said.

"We can create doubts, confuse the public, and use every tool at our disposal. Our survival depends on it," asserted President Williams.

The directors of the CIA and NSA exchanged glances, weighing the gravity of the situation. After a moment's consideration, they nodded in reluctant agreement.

48 CYRUS AND WRECKER'S PLAN TO CRUSH REVOLUTION

At a private spy agency, the command center buzzed with urgency and activity, with agents hunched over computer screens. Colonel Cyrus glanced at multiple monitors displaying surveillance feeds and encrypted files as he spoke on the phone with mercenary crew leader Wrecker.

Colonel Cyrus walked in front of a massive screen showing footage of key global activists rallying supporters and organizing large-scale protests and strikes.

"We've got to neutralize his team ASAP," said Colonel Cyrus.

"He'll be on a train to the East Coast. He'll address the UN shortly after," Wrecker said.

"We should have a contingency plan," said Colonel Cyrus.

"I got your man once, I'll get him again. Just don't let him slip through your fingers," Wrecker said.

"We have to coordinate our teams globally, disrupt their plans, and thwart this revolution once and for all," said Colonel Cyrus.

"I'll sever the head of the snake, and then your global team can restore order and stability," Wrecker replied.

"Keep me posted, Wrecker. This is our chance to reclaim control," Colonel Cyrus said.

49 MATTHEW'S TRAIN RALLY

Matthew's rally train barreled down the tracks. Elijah's chopper, nicknamed, Birdeye flew above it. Two TV news helicopters flew above the train, their cameras capturing the journey live.

In the middle coach, Matthew, Analia, and several followers sat together on one side. The Secretary-General of the United Nations, Mislav Kazimir, a gray-haired, seventy-year-old man - sat across from Matthew. The evangelical leader, Noah, sat next to the Secretary-General. In the head locomotive, Russell, Jackson, and Summer took positions where the lead engineer, a man in his early 40s, and his assistant, a man in his late 30s, operated various high-tech equipment.

In Chicago, a vast crowd stood at the train station, banners and placards held high, eagerly awaiting Matthew's arrival.

Matthew turned to Lee. "What's the security situation at the rallies?" Matthew asked.

Lee activated his earpiece, communicating with Major Russell.

"Major, what's the status at the stations?" Lee asked into the earpiece.

"We can't take any chances. Matthew will have to address the crowd from the train," Russell replied.

Lee looked at Matthew, seeking his approval. Matthew nodded, understanding the necessity. Matthew turned to the Secretary-General.

"Secretary General, do you have any updates regarding my

upcoming address?" Matthew asked.

"We've received some objections from the White House and several other heads of state. They fear it might disrupt the current global order. But most delegates wish to hear your restructuring plan," the Secretary-General said.

"I'd like to have a follow-up meeting with the supportive world leaders to discuss the practical implementation of the plan," said Matthew.

"I'll confirm the date after consulting with the leaders. They recognize the need for a new path forward," said the Secretary-General.

Matthew nodded, acknowledging the Secretary General's words. "Your commitment to peace and belief in the power of compassion gives me hope for humanity," said Matthew.

The Secretary-General smiled warmly and looked up, meeting Matthew's gaze, sharing a moment of connection and purpose.

Noah turned to Matthew, his face revealed a mix of hesitation and anticipation.

"Matthew, you've called for the abolition of organized religion!" Noah said, stumbling over words.

Matthew remained silent momentarily, allowing the weight of the question to settle.

"One needs no religion to believe in God. It's time to eliminate the sources of differences that divide us," Matthew said.

"Hundreds of thousands of priests, rabbis, and imams will be out of work, Matthew," Noah said.

"Houses of worship can be turned into humanitarian centers," Matthew said. "The displaced religious workers can find meaningful work in these centers, continuing their noble service in a different capacity," Matthew continued.

Noah pondered for a moment, trying to process Matthew's words. "Religions give people hope and faith. How can we have faith without the guidance and structure of organized religion?" Noah asked.

"Faith does not require the divisiveness of organized religion. It can exist within the depths of our hearts, nurtured by divine grace," said Matthew.

"We can reform organized religion, Matthew," Noah said.

"Religions have been around for thousands of years. Yet we have neither reformed them nor learned to evolve our souls for the higher dimensions," Matthew said.

"It would be impossible to convince thousands of religious leaders across the country and worldwide," Noah said.

Matthew's voice resonated with conviction, his face exuding wisdom and understanding.

"The time has come for a shift in consciousness, an awakening to the truth that binds us all," said Matthew.

Noah absorbed Matthew's words, his expression a fusion of uncertainty and contemplation.

50 TRAIN ASSAULT AND
LAST-DITCH RESCUE

In the head locomotive, Russell, Summer, and Jackson, vigilant and focused, monitored the train's camera feeds. Suddenly, the screen flickered and went offline.

"What the hell's going on?" Summer asked.

The train engineers checked the equipment, but the system was still offline.

"We need a visual check," Russell said.

Russell, Summer, and Jackson exited the head locomotive. They inspected the vestibules of the train and conversed casually.

"It's too quiet out there," said Summer.

"Are you getting tired of not being shot at?" Jackson asked.

"Birdeye, recon the back end and report," Russell said into his earpiece.

Three of them returned to the head locomotive.

"Suspicious movement, Sir," the chopper reported.

"Identify threats," Russell asked into his earpiece.

"Choppers approaching," the Birdeye reported.

Two menacing helicopters approached the train from behind. The sound of the chopper blades resonated in the air. Enemy chopper #2 fired at the train with rockets, Wrecker commanding the ambush. In the head locomotive, Russell, Jackson, and Summer swiftly dropped to the floor.

"Code Red, Code Red. Birdeye, engage enemy choppers!" Russell shouted into the earpiece.

The coach shook violently, throwing everyone off balance. The windows shattered, showering the compartment with deadly shards of glass.

"Stay down!" Matthew said.

Matthew and several followers sustained minor injuries from the flying glass. Ignoring his wounds, Matthew rushed to help Analia, guiding her to a safer spot on the floor.

Enemy bullets and rockets rained down on the train from multiple directions.

"Fire at will!" Russell shouted into his earpiece.

Enemy chopper #1 targeted a small bridge ahead, firing rockets that exploded, creating a gaping hole in its middle. The Birdeye maneuvered skillfully, evading enemy fire while lining up its target. The gunner aimed and fired two rockets, hitting the first enemy chopper and exploding it in a fiery inferno as it crashed to the ground.

The second enemy chopper maneuvered above the head locomotive, unleashing a barrage of rockets. They exploded on top of the locomotive, engulfing it in flames. The Lead Engineer was struck by sharp debris, which shattered the windshield. The Assistant Engineer checked the lead engineer's pulse. He was dead on the spot.

"No... no..." exclaimed the Assistant Engineer.

Russell and Jackson laid the body of the Lead Engineer on the floor. The Assistant Engineer took charge and kept the train moving forward. As the blazing fire spread toward the interior, Russell and Jackson sustained minor burns to their limbs.

"Damn engine will blow any minute," Summer shouted.

"We have to disengage it from the rest," Jackson said.

The Assistant Engineer desperately engaged the brakes, but they failed. The blazing engine dashed on, unstoppable.

"Damn brakes are on fire!" shouted the Assistant Engineer.

Four of them exited the head locomotive and rushed toward the vestibules.

"Lee, move to the last coach," Russell said into his earpiece.

Jackson and the Assistant Engineer reached underneath the vestibule, frantically trying to disengage the blazing engine. The raging fire reached the middle coach as they failed to disconnect the engine.

"We should detach the last coach," Summer shouted.

Above the train, the news helicopters attempted to capture the unfolding events while avoiding the crossfire. Audiences around the world watched the live TV coverage in horror.

The middle coach was hit by enemy rockets, engulfed in flames, billowing thick smoke into the air. The Assistant Engineer and Jackson rushed to separate the last carriage from the burning coach, flames dancing around them as they struggled. Lee moved Matthew to the last coach of the train.

"Can we evacuate Ana and our guests? Is there a rescue crate?" asked Matthew.

"Major, can the bird drop a crate?" Lee asked into his earpiece.

"Birdeye, drop rescue crate," Russell said.

The blazing train hurtled into a small tunnel. As the train approached the end of the tunnel, the enemy chopper fired a rocket at the front of the train, blowing up the roof. The roofless engine sped toward the blown bridge, dragging two coaches behind it.

"Neutralize the Goddamn chopper now!" Russell shouted into his earpiece.

The Birdeye retaliated with rockets, hitting the enemy chopper. Wrecker jumped with a parachute, vanishing behind the rising inferno. The enemy chopper spun out of control and tumbled, exploding on impact with the river below. At the vestibules, Jackson and the Assistant Engineer continued their frantic efforts to disengage the last coach from the rest of the train. Finally, it was released but dashed on toward the blown bridge.

Russell, Jackson, and Summer quickly entered the last

coach. Amid terror and fear, the coach screeched forward.

"Where's the rescue crate?" Matthew asked tensely.

"What happened to the crate?" Jackson shouted into his earpiece.

"The damn thing's jammed," the pilot replied.

"Forget the crate. Lift the whole freaking coach," Russell said into his earpiece.

The roofless, blazing engine and the second coach reached the blown bridge, tumbling over the edge and plunging into the river below. They exploded upon impact, sending debris flying. The Birdeye hovered above the last coach, its magnetic hoist lowered.

"Hold firm, hoist to engage," the pilot said.

The chopper tried to engage the hoist with the train's metal roof but failed repeatedly. The coach raced onward and plunged over the edge of the blown bridge, revealing the dreadful drop to the river below. Elijah was thrown out of a shattered window, disappearing into the river.

"No… God… no…" Matthew screamed.

Everyone panicked, their faces filled with fear and dismay. Suddenly, a blinding light glowed around Matthew. The coach floated in the air, defying gravity. Mislav and Noah stared at the glowing hands in stunned silence. Noah instinctively performed the Sign of the Cross.

"Forgive me, Lord…" Noah said.

The chopper made one last attempt to engage the magnetic hoist. The hoist finally attached firmly. The helicopter lifted the coach, carrying it away from the impending doom.

51 STEADFAST RESOLVE: MATTHEW REMAINS UNDETERRED

At Matthew's trailer base, the atmosphere was heavy with grief and sadness as Analia wept silently.

"Today, we grieve the loss of a humanitarian who symbolized hope for the world we're trying to build. Let us pray," said Matthew.

The followers joined in the prayer, their heads bowed in reverence.

"May his soul find eternal peace and may his legacy guide us on our journey. Let us remember him not only for his support for the revolution but for the love and the ideals he embodied," Matthew said.

As the prayer ended, the wall screen displayed urgent news updates.

"Breaking News - Millions protest assassination attempts."

"World leaders condemn President Williams."

Russell turned to Matthew with concern etched across his face.

"Matthew, our trip to the United Nations may expose us to further attacks," Russell said.

Matthew closed his eyes for a moment.

"The world awaits my restructuring plan," said Matthew.

Analia, still grieving, interjected with worry in her voice.

"Can you do it virtually?" Analia asked.

Matthew remained silent, his expression pensive.

"You won't stop, and they won't stop until you are dead…" said Analia.

Analia abruptly stood up and walked out, leaving everyone in silence. Russell looked at Matthew's sad but resolute face. Matthew took a deep breath, closing his eyes for a long moment.

"The world has never changed without sacrifices," Matthew said.

Lee hesitated for a moment, his voice barely above a whisper.

"But the Biblical prophecy…" Lee exclaimed.

"It's not a literal kingdom on earth, but a divine realm awakening within us. The End Times can mark the fall of oppression and the rise of a new era. The Millennium Reign isn't about dates — it's a higher state of being. A throne can be the seat of awareness in the human heart. Satan isn't just a being out there — it's the ego, fear, and need for control. When that's silenced and the inner kingdom awakens, the true reign begins. In this age, love becomes the natural order — not by force, but through inner alignment. It's a time of healing and renewal," Matthew said.

"Matthew, you said compassion is the strongest force in the universe. But how does it stand against hate?" Summer asked.

Matthew paused for a moment. "Compassion doesn't fight hate. It absorbs it, transforms it. It shows the hater not who they are, but who they could become."

"You once called humans a symphony of possibilities. What happens when we play the wrong note?" Lee asked.

Matthew replied, "There are no wrong notes — only unresolved chords. Even dissonance serves the song if it returns to harmony. When the inner world finds resonance, the outer world follows. In both the quantum field and the cosmic reality, you are a symphony of possibilities."

"What path must humanity follow when the world is lost in darkness?" Russell asked.

Matthew closed his eyes in silence for a few moments, then spoke softly. "Humanity must find its inner light when everything feels dark. The quiet voice of the soul speaks when the restless noise of the mind stops. The source of creation and liberation lies within our cosmic souls. Our earthly self is but a moment in the timeless vastness of existence. Our eternal struggle is to transcend this realm through awareness of our true spiritual nature. We are both a creation and a creator, for we are part of the Divine and the universal life force."

"Are we approaching the beginning of the Millennium Reign?" Summer asked.

Matthew replied, "Perhaps. But it isn't a fixed point in time. It's a shift in the waveform — a collapse of the old probabilities. The reign of Christ isn't about global governance. It's about quantum coherence across human consciousness."

"Quantum coherence?" Lee whispered.

"Think of human souls as scattered field of particles. But when the inner consciousness is awakened, it's like every soul tuning to the same frequency. Not uniform but harmonized. That's the true reign when free will and divine will vibrate in resonance," Matthew replied.

"So, the binding of the devil within us and the false self... what is that in this reality?" Russell asked.

"It's the decoherence... the collapse of the illusion that we are separate, isolated observers. When that illusion fades, the ego's shadow is neutralized, not by force, but by awareness," Matthew replied.

Summer asked, "Is the Millennium Reign merely prophecy, or is it a pathway into a more evolved state of being?"

Lee added, "And we're not just rediscovering who we are, we're recalibrating, aren't we?"

Matthew nodded, his eyes luminous. "We're at a moment in the multiverse where Earth becomes a sacred node - when every act is entangled with divine intention. A world no longer at war with itself — because consciousness, finally, becomes self-aware and in sync with the universe. Humans live trapped in a single bandwidth of reality. But the soul is multidimensional - part of you traverses in higher dimensions while another part navigates this body and mind. Your existence is an instrument - tuned by memory, emotion, and consciousness. You suffer when you go out of tune. When you love, you resonate."

Summer asked, "How can we rise from the ashes of this global devastation?"

"Not by repeating the past. It means envisioning a world that reflects our inner truths—a civilization built not on scarcity and control, but on coherence and care. When the mind aligns with the soul, society harmonizes. This isn't utopia, it's our true cosmic and quantum nature," Replied Matthew.

The room fell into a deep silence, the weight of Matthew's words hanging in the air, as if the world itself had paused to absorb them. The air pulsed with unspoken revelation, settling into hearts and demanding reflection, not reply.

52 UNFINISHED BUSINESS

Wrecker's SUV sped down a dusty road. The dashboard vibrated with the rough terrain, but he barely noticed. He pushed the accelerator down. His thumb hovered over the phone before the last mile marker had cleared his window.

He dialed Colonel Cyrus on the phone, urgency evident in his voice.

"Colonel, I have to hire a new crew," Wrecker said, skipping any greeting.

A pause at the other end. "The top dog is upset about your failed mission," said Colonel Cyrus.

Wrecker exhaled deeply. "We had a setback, that's all it was." He glanced in the rearview mirror out of habit. "I'll get your man," Wrecker replied.

"The timeline has changed. The exposure has changed," said Colonel Cyrus. "An ambush at the UN is too risky now." There was the soft creak of a leather chair, the distant sound of papers being moved. "Too many eyes on the building since the breach. Security rotations have doubled," Colonel Cyrus said.

"Let me worry about that," Wrecker said. Wrecker's grip tightened on the wheel. He had run operations in tighter windows than this — in worse cities, with worse men, under worse odds. He did not need the Colonel mapping out his obstacles for him. "I know what I'm doing."

"This isn't about doubting your abilities." The Colonel's tone shifted, growing quieter. "There are people above me who are watching this closely. People who don't give second chances. We need this mission to succeed, not almost succeed," Colonel Cyrus said.

"You can count on me, Colonel," Wrecker said. He ended the call before Colonel Cyrus could respond and tossed the phone onto the passenger seat.

53 MATTHEW UNVEILS
RESTRUCTURING PLAN AT THE UN

A helicopter gracefully descended onto the helipad at the UN headquarters in New York City. Matthew, accompanied by his followers, stepped out of the helicopter. Russell and his team stood guard at the entrance, their gazes focused and vigilant. UN security operatives, strategically positioned around the UN building, kept a watchful eye on the surroundings, ensuring the safety of the event.

Matthew and his team entered a massive convention hall abuzz with activity. Scores of journalists, equipped with cameras and microphones, filled the room. Monitors and screens displayed the live feed of the event. The Secretary-General stepped onto the podium, bearing the United Nations emblem.

"Distinguished dignitaries, it is my distinct privilege to welcome Matthew," said the Secretary-General.

The delegates and journalists greeted Matthew with applause. The Secretary-General took his seat beside Matthew. The UN staffers distributed copies of Matthew's restructuring Plan to the seated delegates, their name tags indicating their respective nations. The brief outlines of the Plan were also projected onto a massive wall screen. The delegates eagerly examined the visionary Plan, their faces filled with curiosity and anticipation.

"Thank you for being here on this auspicious Human Rights Day. The Plan before you lays out a decade-long process for restructuring the world," said Matthew.

The US Ambassador addressed Matthew with a blunt hint of skepticism.

"You have called for the abolition of religion and redistribution of natural resources of this planet. To some of us, it sounds like an absurd utopia. With all due respect, I believe your utopian idealism is your fatal flaw," said the US Ambassador.

Matthew remained silent for a moment, his voice calm yet commanding.

"If an idea is not absurd at first, there's no hope for it. Albert Einstein said it so prophetically. Utopianism is what we need for such ideas that have been considered long before me but were always discredited by the deceptive disinformation of the rulers," said Matthew.

Many delegates broke out in applause, expressing their support for Matthew's words. Others pondered in silence, considering the implications.

"How can we possibly redistribute the natural resources of this world?" asked the British Ambassador.

"The vast natural resources are like the air we breathe and the sunlight we use. All humans have a natural right to these God-given resources. This right is a human right. A fair redistribution of natural resources can alleviate the enduring mass poverty and obscene inequality that plague our world," replied Matthew.

"Are you going to be the supreme leader of this so-called One World?" asked the Australian Ambassador.

"I'm here not to be a leader of anything but to avert the self-destructive path the world is on," Matthew replied.

"It all sounds good in theory, but transforming more than two hundred countries into a one-world structure would be impossible," the Chinese Ambassador said.

"The crucial first step in the transformative Plan is to

111

reform the UN itself and to abolish organized religion and organized politics. Once these critical changes are accomplished, we can embark on a comprehensive process to restructure all other aspects of the world," Matthew said.

The convention hall was filled with murmurs and whispers as the delegates began to process the implications of Matthew's words.

At the UN entrance, Russell and Summer stood guard. Russell hesitated, pausing briefly before speaking.

"Maybe we can take a vacation after all. Can we start over?" asked Russell.

Summer's eyes widened slightly, surprise mingling with hope. She looked deeply into his eyes, longing and uncertainty in her gaze.

"For what it's worth, you're the only one who brought me down to the real world," said Summer.

Russell took a step closer to Summer, bridging the gap between them.

"I have been thinking about giving up this life of combat," Russell said.

Summer's lips curved into a loving smile, tears of joy filling her eyes.

At the rear of the UN building, Wrecker emerged with two soldiers in stolen uniforms, blending in with the UN security forces. They made their way toward the helipad and opened fire at the chopper. At the UN entrance, chaos erupted as Russell reacted.

"Evacuate Matthew! Move! Move!" Russell shouted.

Russell and his operatives sprinted toward the helipad, engaging Wrecker's forces. Wrecker was struck by a bullet, causing him to stumble and fall to the ground. His soldiers retaliated, returning fire. Matthew and his followers rushed through a narrow emergency exit corridor, seeking cover behind crates and walls as the sound of gunfire intensified.

At the helipad, Russell and his troops neutralized and zip-cuffed Wrecker and his soldiers. Matthew and his followers rushed to the helipad and boarded the chopper. The helicopter prepared for takeoff, blades spinning loudly. Matthew turned back and walked toward Wrecker, kneeling beside him. He laid his right hand on Wrecker's wounds as he groaned in pain. As Wrecker's wounds healed, his stone-cold eyes turned tranquil with disbelief. Matthew whispered with compassion.

"May God forgive you," Matthew said.

As the chopper ascended into the night sky, Wrecker lay on the ground, transformed by the encounter with the divine.

54 MATTHEW CALLS FOR WHITE HOUSE BLOCKADE

Matthew and his followers gathered in the trailer base, their eyes fixed on the rapidly flashing news headlines.

"Breaking News - President Williams Orders the UN to Leave US Soil."

"Breaking News - President Williams Considers Using Nuclear Weapons in Foreign Wars."

The footage displayed protests raging across the country and worldwide, revealing a global outcry against the President's actions.

"It's time to blockade the White House. The President's actions have crossed all boundaries," Matthew said.

"I've been waiting for this moment. I would love nothing more than to drag him out of the White House," said Lee.

"We can't fly our choppers near the White House. We must proceed carefully and find another way," Russell said.

Matthew nodded, acknowledging Russell's concerns. The wall screen displayed footage of worldwide protests swelling in size and fervor.

"Let us pray," Matthew said. The followers bowed their heads in prayer, seeking guidance for the journey ahead.

55 SEEKING REDEMPTION: WRECKER EMBRACES A NEW PATH

Wrecker picked up a sturdy shovel and walked to the cemetery behind his farmhouse. He stopped before his wife's grave and put the shovel beside him. Emotion welled up as he gazed at the headstone.

"I'm sorry for all the pain I've caused. It's time for me to let go of this life," Wrecker whispered.

He picked up the shovel and dug a fresh grave. He entered the old, weathered barn and walked toward a dusty workbench where two military-grade weapons cases lay. He lifted them one by one, taking a deep breath.

He walked back to the freshly dug grave and gently placed the weapons cases inside, the final remnants of his violent past now laid to rest. He poured gasoline onto the cases and took a lighter out of his pocket. He turned the lighter on, its flame flickering in the darkness. With a determined throw, he hurled the lighter into the grave, setting the weapons cases ablaze.

He watched the blaze, transfixed by the consuming fire. After a long moment, he took the shovel in hand and filled the grave with gravel and soil until all traces of the fire were hidden beneath the earth. Standing tall, leaning on the shovel, Wrecker gazed at the newly covered grave, a chapter of his life had come to an end.

56 PROTESTERS STORM THE WHITE HOUSE

Thousands of protesters blockaded the White House. The crowd broke into thunderous cheers as Matthew and his team arrived in a convoy of three SUVs on the road outside the White House. Matthew addressed the crowd using a megaphone.

"My brothers and sisters, I call upon all police, military, and mercenary forces to lay down your weapons and join our revolution," said Matthew.

Multiple news helicopters hovered above, capturing the momentous event from a distance. As tension grew, the government forces responded by deploying tear gas to disperse the protesters. The enraged crowd began hurling bricks and rocks at the guards. The guards fired with live bullets, wounding and killing several protesters, adding fuel to the raging anger. The White House rooftop security forces fired rockets at Matthew's convoy, setting two of the vehicles ablaze. Analia pulled Matthew inside the remaining vehicle.

"We must go! It's too dangerous!" said Analia.

The protesters and activists erupted in furious rage, storming the White House. Russell, Jackson, Summer, and Lee joined the activists in leading the siege. Matthew stepped out of the vehicle and followed them.

"No… Matthew!" Analia screamed.

Russell looked back at Matthew.

"You should stay here," Russell said.

"I can't hide away," said Matthew.

Matthew tenderly guided Analia into the vehicle, carefully closing the door behind her. He signaled the security operatives as they surrounded it, standing guard. Matthew moved forward, resolute in his purpose.

Inside the White House hallways, Russell and his team clashed with the government security forces as they advanced toward the underground vault. The activists shielded Matthew as they took cover and moved forward carefully.

At the underground vault entrance, several secret service officers rushed President Williams and his team to the Emergency Operation Center. Inside the vault, the wall screens displayed the chaotic scenes inside and outside the White House.

"What are my options?" asked President Williams.

"Our country is tearing itself apart, and the world is on the brink," replied Vice President Madison.

"Mr. President, we need to make a decision," said CIA Director Miles.

"Do you want me to resign? I'm beginning to think you misled me deliberately," said President Williams.

"With all due respect, I resent that accusation, Mr. President," said CIA Director Miles.

"It'd be wise to resign gracefully rather than being removed by the mob. It would prevent further escalation," NSA Director Collin suggested.

The President paced back and forth, his eyes fixed on the live news feeds, showing violent clashes and protests spreading across the country and beyond.

"I think the only way to salvage your presidency is to launch a false flag operation and further escalate the foreign wars," said CIA Director Miles.

President Williams looked at the NSA Director and the

Vice President. The NSA Director nodded, silently giving his agreement. The Vice President remained silent and uncommitted. President Williams stared at her, disappointment in his face. He paused for a moment, then nodded.

"We could deploy our stealth nuclear missiles, targeting the war zones," said CIA Director Miles.

"I'm not convinced that's a wise move, Sir," said Vice President Madison.

President Williams turned his attention to Vice President Madison, his expression hardened.

"You got a better plan?" asked President Williams.

The Vice President hesitated, contemplating her response, but ultimately remained silent. President Williams led the team to the War Room, where the military leaders awaited, ready to discuss the plan further.

57 NUCLEAR NIGHTMARE: MATTHEW AVERTS APOCALYPSE

Russell and his team engaged in a fierce battle with the security forces at the underground vault entrance, finally disarming the guards outside the vault.

Matthew approached the guards.

"Please open the door," said Matthew.

"We can't do that, Sir," said the male guard.

"It requires multi-level security protocol, including the President's retina scan," said the female guard.

Jackson stepped forward, pressing his gun against the chest of the male guard.

"Is there any way to bypass the protocol?" Jackson shouted.

"No, Sir," replied the male guard.

In the War Room, General Garrison stood at the control panel. Rows of monitors displayed maps, satellite images, and live feeds from various military bases and installations.

"Mr. President, it's your call, but in my view, it might just trigger World War Three," said General Garrison.

The Vice President's face paled with fear and uncertainty, realizing the gravity of the situation.

"Sir, the ramifications could be catastrophic. We should consider all possible alternatives before we take such drastic measures," said Vice President Madison.

President Williams pondered the weight of his decision, his jaw tightened, and his brow furrowed with concern. He glanced at the faces of those present.

"If it saves my presidency, let's start World War Three. We'll deal with the aftermath later. Initiate the launch!" said President Williams.

The General's eyes widened, but he quickly regained composure and nodded. President Williams moved to the control panel, his hands shaking slightly as he entered the launch codes. The room fell into an uneasy silence as the monitors showed the nuclear missiles activating and counting down T-30.

At the underground vault entrance, Russell and his team pointed their guns at the security guards. Matthew stepped closer to the guards, his aura exuding compassion and serenity.

"Please open it," asked Matthew.

The male operative glanced at his fellow guard, who shared a conflicted look.

"My dear brother and sister, we must stop this nuclear apocalypse that could bring about the annihilation of humanity," said Matthew.

"We have our orders, Sir. No one gets through without proper authorization. The President's safety is our top priority," said the male guard.

"Even if we wanted to, we don't have the authority to open the gate without proper clearance," said the female guard.

"Your humanity must rise above the orders given by men. This is not just about the President's safety. This is about the survival of all of us," said Matthew.

"We're powerless to act without clearance," said the female guard.

Russell and Jackson grew impatient as they cocked their guns, pointing them at the guards.

"Time is running out! Open the fucking door!" said

Jackson.

Matthew reached out and gently touched the male guard's arm. "We must find a way to do the right thing for the preservation of humanity," said Matthew.

The guards exchanged one last glance, their resolve faltering under Matthew's persuasive words. With a deep breath, the female guard nodded to her fellow operative. They hesitated momentarily, then entered codes into the security panel. A secret compartment opened as they pressed two hidden buttons, exposing a small, intricate device. The guard placed the device against a scanner next to the vault. The vault clicked, disengaging its locks. The heavy metal door started to creak open, revealing the entrance to the bunker. Jackson and Summer swiftly secured the guards with zip cuffs.

Matthew and his team entered the vault, storming into the War Room. Russell and his operatives quickly surrounded the room, pointing their guns at the leaders sitting and standing around. Jackson strode forward, his gaze fixed on the President. He raised his gun, pressing it firmly against the President's forehead. Gasps and murmurs rippled through the room.

"This ends now!" said Jackson.

The President met Jackson's gaze, his glare hardened, his expression defiant. The launch monitors showed the countdown T-15. Matthew stepped forward to the nuclear launch platform.

"Please abort the launch!" said Matthew.

The operative turned to the General and the President, waiting for their response.

"Deploy as ordered!" President Williams shouted.

Matthew glanced around the nuclear launch platform. The launch monitor showed the countdown T-5.

Matthew closed his eyes and raised both his hands. A blinding light emanated from his palms, casting a radiant glow around him. The countdown froze abruptly at T-2, interrupted by a small explosion setting the console ablaze. The leaders stared in stunned awe at Matthew's glowing hands and the spreading fire, their faces etched with fear and disbelief.

Russell's operatives disarmed the President's team. Matthew and his followers, accompanied by the bewildered leaders, exited the vault and arrived on the White House deck.

58 MATTHEW'S LAST STAND: A CALL FOR PEACE

The deck and the surrounding area were filled with a sea of people, signs, and placards held high. Matthew and his team escorted the leaders onto the deck. The crowd erupted into rapturous cheers and chants. Matthew stepped forward commanding the crowd's attention. As the cheers subsided, Matthew addressed the crowd.

"Let us forgive those who have lost their way. They will be held accountable for their actions," said Matthew.

The crowd broke into thunderous applause, their chants growing louder. Signs reading "Matthew for President" and "God Bless Matthew" are raised high.

"A United Nations Special Council should be formed to initiate the restructuring process. In our homeland, I implore all separatist factions to lay down their arms, to end the civil war, and to join us in the pursuit of peace and justice for all," Matthew said.

President Williams, consumed by anger and vengeance, stared at Matthew with hatred. Suddenly, he managed to grab Summer's gun. With a trembling hand, he aimed it directly at

Matthew and pulled the trigger.

The crowd gasped in shock, and chaos erupted. Russell reacted swiftly, shooting President Williams in the heart. The President dropped to the ground, lifeless.

The crowd fell into a stunned silence, their eyes fixed on the fallen Matthew. Some began to weep and sob. Television reporters, capturing every moment, transmitted the shocking scene to the world.

Analia stepped out of the vehicle and ran to the White House deck. She knelt beside Matthew, holding his head in her lap. Tears streamed down her face.

"The world needs you... I need you," Analia whispered through tears.

Matthew's vision flickered, his consciousness fading. He caught glimpses of Analia's face through blurred eyes.

"The world needs the path I showed," Matthew hoarsely whispered.

He took a shaky breath, his strength waning. Analia's sobs intensified, her grief consuming her.

"I'll see you," Matthew said in a barely audible voice.

Matthew took his final breath, his eyes fixed on Analia's tear-streaked face. She wept, cradling his lifeless body. The crowd remained silent, unable to comprehend the tragedy that had unfolded before them.

59 UN HONORS MATTHEW: POSTHUMOUS NOBEL PEACE PRIZE

One year later...

The vast assembly hall in the UN headquarters was filled with dignitaries. Analia sat in the front row alongside Matthew's disciples, their faces filled with sorrow. Analia's eyes welled up with tears as she gazed at the podium where Matthew once stood. With a deep breath, she stepped onto the podium.

"This is a dark time for humanity as we mourn an immeasurable loss for our world. But in this moment of grief, we must find the strength to continue the work Matthew started," said Analia.

Her voice resonated throughout the hall, capturing the hearts of the delegates. They broke into applause, expressing their support and solidarity.

A UN staffer approached the Secretary-General, leaning in to whisper. The Secretary-General nodded in acknowledgment. The large wall screen behind the podium came to life, revealing a live broadcast of the Nobel Committee's press conference. On the screen, a man in his late 70s, the Chairperson of the Nobel Committee, appeared.

"Ladies and gentlemen, the Norwegian Nobel Committee

has made a rare departure from our longstanding policy regarding posthumous awards. In recognition of his relentless work and contribution to humanity, this year's Nobel Peace Prize is being posthumously conferred upon Matthew," said the Nobel Committee Chairperson.

A collective gasp rippled through the assembly hall. Analia, fighting back tears, joined the dignitaries in a standing ovation. As the applause gradually subsided, Analia clutched her hands together.

"This recognition serves as a testament to the indelible mark Matthew left in our hearts. It is a reminder that his vision for peace and justice transcends his physical presence. We must carry forth his torch with unswerving resolve," concluded Analia.

60 DIVINE TOUCH RENEWS
ANALIA'S RESOLVE

Analia drifted into a deep sleep, resting her head on the computer desk. The screen displayed a TV reporter in her 30s broadcasting from the field.

"Acting on Matthew's transformative plans, the United Nations has successfully brokered peace accords in embattled regions of the world. The long-awaited reorganization process has begun, and the world is slowly healing from the scars of conflict," said the reporter. The footage showed images of rebuilding efforts, scenes of people coming together, and cities rising from the ashes.

Suddenly, engulfed in a radiant light, Matthew appeared, laying a gentle hand on Analia's head. She stirred in her sleep, sensing a divine presence. She lifted her head, her eyes widening in astonishment as she saw Matthew standing before her.

"You're not done yet, Ana," said Matthew.

Analia's eyes welled up with tears, her voice trembling.

"This wasn't how I wanted to end this journey. You left me here alone. I don't know if I can continue," Analia said.

Matthew maintained a serene expression, radiating compassion.

"You're never alone, I'm with you. You have the will to carry on, to fulfill the purpose within your heart," said Matthew.

The divine light enveloped Analia as Matthew slowly faded away. Analia's tears flowed freely as she wept silently for a while. She sat up straight, wiping her tears away. She reached for the keyboard, her fingers trembling slightly, her words flowing, each keystroke imbued with passion.

She concluded the chronicle of his extraordinary odyssey, as humanity moved forward into a world forever transformed by the divine resurgence he ignited.